Divine and H
and Other S

»»»»»»»» «««««««««

Leo Tolstoy

Divine and Human

and Other Stories

TRANSLATED FROM THE RUSSIAN
AND WITH AN INTRODUCTION AND NOTES
BY GORDON SPENCE

NORTHWESTERN UNIVERSITY PRESS
EVANSTON, ILLINOIS

»»»»»»»» «««««««««

Northwestern University Press
Evanston, Illinois 60208-4210

English translation, compilation, and introduction copyright © 2000 by
Northwestern University Press. Published 2000. All rights reserved.

Printed in the United States of America
10 9 8 7 6 5 4 3 2
ISBN 0-8101-1762-2

Library of Congress Cataloging-in-Publication Data

Tolstoy, Leo, graf, 1828–1910.
    [Short stories. English. Selections]
    Divine and human and other stories / Leo Tolstoy ; translated from the
Russian and with an introduction and notes by Gordon Spence.
        p.   cm.
    ISBN 0-8101-1762-2 (alk. paper)
    1. Tolstoy, Leo, graf, 1828–1910—Translations into English. I. Spence, G. W.
(Gordon William) II. Title.
PG3366.A15 S68 2000
891.73'3—dc21   00-008021

»»» CONTENTS «««

All royalties from this book will be given to Amnesty International. The only prisoner of conscience in these three stories is a religious schismatic, since the other political prisoners all used violence or planned to do so, but other concerns of Amnesty International appear in two of the stories: torture by flogging and the death penalty.

The stories are relevant to the present time because they deal with issues that still concern us, but this is not the only reason why a translation of them is offered to the public. They are among the last works of a great man and deserve to be known by readers who cannot read Russian. Milton said in *Areopagitica* that a good book is the precious lifeblood of a master spirit. To read Tolstoy closely, turning his sentences into English as accurately as is compatible with readability, is to have at least the illusion of coming close to his spirit and enabling others to approach it, too. This needs to be mentioned now when people like to repeat the saying that as institution the author is dead. Tolstoy's opinion was to the contrary; he believed that through a work of literary art an author communicated his feelings to others.[1] Further, if we receive those feelings when reading, we shall know how deplorable is the contempt in some progressive quarters for the study of works by so-called dead white European male writers. It is as deplorable as Tolstoy's rejection, for reasons of his own, of the works of the Greek tragedians and Aristophanes, Dante, Tasso, Shakespeare,

Milton, and Ibsen.[2] Such writers are not dead in the sense that matters and will live till the future dares forget the past. So it is to be hoped that Tolstoy's spirit can be conveyed to readers of his works, and even if we disagree with him, or with other great writers of the past, on points of doctrine or belief, we should understand that neglect of them would only impoverish us because it would deprive us of something of the power of humanity.

The translations of the stories are based on the texts printed in volume 11 of the twelve-volume edition of Tolstoy's collected works edited by S. A. Makashin and L. D. Opulskaya and published in Moscow in 1987. I should thank the Syndics of Cambridge University Library for permission to reprint in the appendix my translation, which was made from a microfilm provided by that library, of excerpts from Sergei Maximov's *Siberia and Penal Servitude*. I am grateful to Alexandra Smith for checking a considerable part of my translation of "Divine and Human" and showing how I should make some corrections, and I should like to thank Tatiana Blagova for helping me with some obsolete words in "What For?" and some colloquial expressions in "Berries." I am especially grateful to both these scholars for the encouragement that they have given me in this work. Needless to say, if any errors remain, they are my fault, not theirs. I should thank Janet Bray for finding out the Ukrainian spelling of some place names and Christina Stachurski for help with proofreading. I am also indebted to Peter Low for explaining a French expression, to Mark Williams for information about the Catholic mass, and to Alexandra Smith and Anne Taylor for some direction about the streets of St. Petersburg.

As for the spelling of Russian names, I have transliterated the Cyrillic (though without marking the soft signs) except in the case of emperors and an empress, where I have used the English equivalents, and I have written our author's name not as "Lev Tolstoi" but as "Leo Tolstoy," which is how he wrote it in the Roman alphabet. I have used Polish spelling for the Polish names, except for Warsaw and Cracow.

This book is dedicated to my son, Andrew, and my daughter, Catherine.

Gordon Spence

The three stories contained in this book were all written by Tolstoy around the time of the Russian revolution of 1905. The first of them to be composed, "Divine and Human" (drafted in the first half of 1904 and revised near the close of the following year), deals directly with revolutionaries, though not those of the first decade of the twentieth century.[1] It looks back to the populists of the 1870s and the program of political assassination that culminated in the murder of the emperor Alexander II in 1881. Tolstoy's conception of the story began with an interest in the execution of terrorists in Odessa in 1879 and with the idea of bringing together a revolutionary and a religious schismatic in prison.[2] In the story he shows the futility of political assassination by means of contrasts. One contrast is between terrorism and Christianity, as this religion is understood by a converted terrorist in his cell and by an Old Believer who is persecuted for his faith. The other is between terrorism and the Marxist theory of the tendency of economic laws to determine the structure of society, this latter contrast being developed in a dramatic clash between a terrorist and a group of Marxists exiled in Siberia. "Berries," which was written in two days in June 1905, contrasts the tiresome and inane conversation of liberals with the innocence of peasant children.[3] Tolstoy noted in his diary on October 23 that "the frivolity of the people who are making this revolution is astonishing and disgusting: childishness without the innocence of children." His celebration of the innocence of peasant children shows by implication how far astray from the truth the revolutionaries and the government had wandered in their conflict. "What For?" wh h was written early in 1906, is a historical tale, dealing with one ːmily's suffering in consequence of the Polish insurrection of 1830 to 1831 but showing this suffering as typical of the persecution of Polish patriots.[4] By protesting in the story against the oppressive measures of Nicholas I, emperor of Russia and king of Poland, Tolstoy condemns the autocracy, whose disastrous policies in the nineteenth century brought Russia to the crisis of a revolution. All three stories were included in Tolstoy's miscellaneous publication, *A Circle of Reading,* in 1906.[5]

In 1905 Tolstoy reached the age of seventy-seven. It is rare to find a writer at that age not only so productive, but also so acute, concise, and profound in his composition. Most of the great works of his last period were behind him. *Resurrection,* the novel in which he gave his definitive view of the iniquitous conditions of Russian society of his time, had been published in 1899. Despite all the essays and treatises that he wrote in his last years, the urge to create works of fiction did not leave him. He continued to extend his imaginative sympathies and to strive for clarity, brevity, and sharpness of style in his fictions. "Divine and Human" and "What For?" both contain a great deal in a small space, and their narratives move swiftly. In both, the essential action is internal, occurring in the minds of the prisoners in "Divine and Human" and in the heart of the heroine in "What For?" while the descriptions of the external world are vivid, whether they are of a dull autumnal morning in Odessa as a prisoner is taken to execution or of a bright spring morning in Saratov as a Polish family attempts to escape from exile. In "Berries" both description and comic narrative serve to contrast the empty lives of the gentry with the labor of the peasants, who live in close touch with nature.

By "Tolstoy's last period" is meant the period that began with the writing of his *Confession* in 1879. This work is an account of his search for the meaning of life, undertaken when, despite his fame, his prosperity, and the many interests of his life, he was tempted to commit suicide. He emerged from this crisis with the resolution to discover for himself the truth of Christianity, as distinct from the doctrines of the Orthodox Church, and to give up his privileges as one of the gentry who lived on the backs of the people, renouncing his property and joining the peasants in labor for the support of life. His marriage prevented the satisfactory fulfillment of the latter part of this resolution, but he wrote eloquent treatises in condemnation of the government and the existing social order in Russia and Western Europe, as well as essays on religious philosophy and expositions of Christian teaching. In *What I Believe,* published in 1884, he announced that the key to the Christian teaching was the command of nonresistance to evil by violence in the Sermon on the Mount. In *What Then Must We Do?* (1886) he dealt with the problem of economic oppression, coming to very radical conclusions, and he carried this radicalism further in *The Kingdom of God Is within You* (1893–94), where, in view of the present condition of Europe with its social injustices, its armed nations on the brink of war, and the threat of violent revolution, the doctrine of nonresistance is advocated as a total refusal to recognize the state. Meanwhile, in the treatise *On Life* (1888) he expounded a philosophy whereby the Platonic dualism of body and soul appeared in a new form, as he maintained that our real self is not the "animal personality," which can only ever obtain unreal phantoms of happiness and which preys on others, but that the real self is "reasonable consciousness," which is beyond time and space and in which all people can become united through the growth of spiritual love. True life, according to this doctrine, requires the renunciation of the illusory good of the animal personality and the subordination of this personality to the law of reason.

Such an understanding of true life is reached by Svetlogub, a revolutionary populist in "Divine and Human," when he reads the Gospels alone in his cell. Svetlogub is modeled partly on Dmitrii Lizogub, who was hanged in Odessa on August 10, 1879, who was described in *Narodnaya Volya*—the periodical of the revolutionary organization called the People's Will—as "a figure of quite outstanding spiritual grandeur," and who smiled when taken to the gallows.[6] But there were important parts of Lizogub's life that Tolstoy did not use. In creating the fictitious character, Tolstoy has, first, made Svetlogub an example of one of the intellectuals who "went to the people" in 1874 and who, on being defeated in their attempts to instigate a revolution by propaganda, resorted to acts of terror against senior officers of the state and, above all, the emperor. Second, Tolstoy has made Svetlogub's approach to the Gospels similar to his own. Svetlogub places a Tolstoyan emphasis on the five commandments of the Sermon on the Mount, and like Tolstoy he rejects whatever is miraculous or obscure in the Gospels. Yet there is a significant difference between the mental state of the converted Svetlogub and what Tolstoy considered to be essential to a true understanding of life, and this is that Svetlogub does not repent of his use of violence in the past, saying that he could not have acted differently. This is psychologically convincing, however, for as a revolutionary who has devoted himself wholly to the cause of the people, he sees himself and his comrades as the salt of the earth, rejoicing in the sacrifice that he has made.

The old schismatic in "Divine and Human" is based on a personal acquaintance of Tolstoy's, an Old Believer named Mikhail

Maximov, who was often at Yasnaya Polyana, Tolstoy's home, and whose nickname was Tobacco Power.[7] The religious quest of the old schismatic in the story is described with great sympathy, even though it is based on the Revelation of St. John, which Tolstoy had previously dismissed with contempt. In his "Introduction to an Examination of the Gospels" (written about 1880) Tolstoy had declared that the Book of Revelation revealed absolutely nothing.[8] Yet in "Divine and Human" he shows how for the old schismatic the imagery of that book represents not only the ground of his rejection of the Russian church and state, but also his understanding of the true life that transcends the death of the body.

The clash between Mezhenetskii, another terrorist in "Divine and Human," and a group of Marxists is of great historical interest. The populists of the 1870s were acquainted with Marxism, but their endeavor was to develop socialism in Russia on the basis of the existing village communes, in the hope that their country could avoid passing through the bourgeois–capitalist stage of development. For this reason they were in a hurry to promote a revolution, before capitalism and industry became established on a large scale. Their success, however, in assassinating the emperor in 1881 was also a failure, since it was not followed by any popular uprising, but provoked a severe political reaction under Alexander III. Plekhanov, who became known as the father of Russian Marxism, had been a populist opposed to the use of terror. In Geneva in 1883 he formed the first revolutionary organization of Russian Marxists, the Group for the Liberation of Labor, composed at that date of five people, and there he wrote books criticizing populism and advocating Marxism. These would presumably have been read by the Marxists whom Mezhenetskii met at Krasnoyarsk in about 1887. Mezhenetskii was unlucky to have fallen among imprisoned Marxists at that date, since the first congress of the Russian Social Democratic Labor Party, which was a revolutionary party founded by nine Marxists, was not held until 1898. But Marxism gained ground with the development of capitalism and industry in Russia in the 1880s and 1890s. Populism, however, had its survivors and heirs, who formed the Socialist Revolutionary Party at the turn of the century, and the Combat Organization of this party returned to the policy of assassination.[9]

In an article entitled "Thou Shalt Not Kill," written in 1900 but prohibited in Russia, Tolstoy explained the absurdity of political assassination, though censuring the rulers who commanded armies more severely than the revolutionaries who occasionally murdered those rulers, and he said that the thing to do was not to kill the kings, emperors, and presidents, but to cease to support the arrangement of society of which they were a result.[10] In "A Great Iniquity," published in *Russkaya Mysl* (*Russian Thought*) in 1905, he argued that liberals, Social Democrats, and Socialist Revolutionaries were all mistaken in trying to change the political order without abolishing the chief evil under which the people suffered: private ownership of the land. At the conclusion of this essay he expressed his disapproval of the Marxist program that is set forth by Roman in "Divine and Human":

> I think that the Russian people should not be proletarianized in imitation of the peoples of Europe and America, but should on the contrary solve the land question at home by the abolition of private ownership, and should show other people the path to a reasonable, free, and happy life (outside industrial, factory, and capitalistic violence and slavery)—in which its great and historic vocation lies.[11]

The idea that the Russian people have such a vocation seems to have been taken from the Slavophiles, who opposed the Westernizers in Russia in the nineteenth century.

In "Divine and Human" the human is represented by the defeat of Mezhenetskii, and the divine by Svetlogub's and the old schismatic's discovery of true life. Svetlogub in his last hours feels raised above the world, and the old man's death with his apocalyptic vision is described as the greatest thing in the world. The story thus conforms to the religious teaching that Tolstoy worked out in answer to his question of the meaning of life. For mortal, finite life can have meaning only in relation to the immortal, infinite life of the spirit, the discovery of which is recorded in the tale. In contrast, "What For?" asks a question to which it does not give any reply. The question is Albina's: What is all this suffering for? What is its purpose? Tolstoy answered, or thought he answered, this question in his treatise *On Life,* saying that the function of suffering was to prove to us that our true life was not the life of our personalities and that we could accept suffering and allay it by living in conformity with reasonable consciousness: "Only when, being man, he descends to the level of an animal, does he see death and suffering. Death and sufferings, like bogies, then hoot at him from all sides and goad him into taking the one available road of human life subject to his law of reason and expressing itself in love."[12] The absence from "What For?" of any implication of this ascetic answer shows how far the story departs from Tolstoy's religious philosophy.

Yet in its protest against the oppressive policy of Nicholas I the story is typical of its author. For when Tolstoy was most concerned as a social critic he made statements that contradicted his religious philosophy. This was inevitable, because his social criticism was motivated by compassion and indignation—compassion for those whose animal personalities were degraded or destroyed by the social system, and indignation at the perpetrators of injustice. Having formed a philosophy that denied the intrinsic value of the personality, he was bound to contradict that philosophy when protesting against injustices and oppression. As Plekhanov put it, "Tolstoy was not always a Tolstoyan. . . . Tolstoy appeared to his contemporaries to be a great teacher of life only when he repudiated his own teaching about life."[13] There is a particularly clear self-contradiction on the subject of rights. In *What I Believe* Tolstoy said, in accordance with his principle of self-renunciation, that we should understand that we had no rights but only oblig-ations to God, and he repeated this in his diary on April 2, 1906.[14] But when dealing with the land question he repeatedly affirmed that everyone had a natural right to obtain subsistence from the land. In "A Great Iniquity" the evil complained of was that most people were deprived of the natural right of everyone to have the use of a portion of the land on which they were born.[15] Natural rights do not have any basis in Tolstoy's religious philosophy, but they come from his instinctive sense of justice.

In "What For?" "joy of life" is a key term. The joy referred to is the joy of earthly life, which, unlike the true life of the spirit, is very vulnerable. Albina is deprived of it through the tragic action of the tale. The sadness of her loss is due to our sense that she had a right to that joy, but the discovery that is made at the climax of this tale echoes the terrible truth revealed in some Greek tragedies, that human happiness is an illusion, as is declared, for example, by the chorus in *King Oedipus*.[16]

This is the revelation of what Tolstoy called the fundamental contradiction of human life, consisting in the realization that although everyone seeks their own happiness, personal happiness proves to be impossible.[17] In the treatise *On Life* he tried to show that we could resolve this contradiction by subordinating the ani-mal personality to the law of reason, but as we read "What For?" we feel that it would be insulting to Albina to tell her that she is at the level of an animal and that her suffering is to teach her to submit to the law of reason. She is not a sage; she wants to live a normal human life, and for such a person there is no solution to the fundamental contradiction with which she is confronted.

Although Albina's question is not answered in the story, the cause of her suffering is made plain. It consists in the oppressive policy of Nicholas I and in Albina's and her husband's courageous refusal to submit to that policy. The story is written from the point of view of Polish patriotism and is therefore at variance with Tolstoy's own opinion of patriotism. In "Christianity and Patriotism," written in 1894 about the Franco-Russian celebrations, Tolstoy denounced patriotism as a state of mind produced among the people by schools, the church, and a venal press for purposes required by the government and as a temporary excitement aroused among unthinking portions of the population by the ruling classes. He added: "The patriotism of oppressed nationalities is no exception to this. That too is unnatural in the laboring masses, and is artificially fostered in them by the upper classes."[18] But through the study of historical sources Tolstoy was able to give a sympathetic presentation of the patriotism of the Polish gentry. This was facilitated by the fact that he shared their hostility to Nicholas I, who is a target in his novella *Hadji Murad*.

When Albina first asks her question "What for?" on the death of her children, she thinks: "Józio and I—we don't want anything from anyone, except for him to live as he was born to and as his forefathers lived, and for me only—to live with him, love him, love my little ones, and bring them up." This shows the limitation of her point of view. Józef Migurski was born into the Polish gentry (the *szlachta*), and Albina thinks that he has a right to live as one of that class, even though it exploited the peasants. Quoting an English traveler on the wretchedness of the Polish serfs at the time of the insurrection, R. F. Leslie shows that both the "Code Napoléon" in the duchy of Warsaw and the structure of the Polish kingdom that was set up by the Congress of Vienna had deplorable effects on the relations between landlords and peasants.[19] Albina seems quite unaware of this social problem, which does not enter the story; but a reader familiar with the history of that time will recognize that for Migurski to live as he was born to he would benefit from such a system of land ownership as Tolstoy considered to be iniquitous. Such a reader will also know that the Polish government in 1830 to 1831 had great difficulty in getting any support from the peasants in the insurrection against the Russians. Leslie quotes some peasants in the palatinate of Cracow who said: "We will march against the Muscovite, but first we will cut down the *szlachta* because they are the cause of our misery."[20] In order to maintain an unqualified sympathy with Albina, therefore, Tolstoy has not only set aside his own religious philosophy, but has also excluded his own concern with social justice and the rights of the peasants.

His sympathy with the peasants is clear in "Berries." This story shows the value of life that is lived in harmony with nature and so is related to an aspect of Tolstoy's religious thought that is not formulated in his treatise *On Life*. In spite of the dualism of "reasonable consciousness" and "animal personality" that is expounded in that essay, and which assigns only an instrumental value to the body, making it a mere tool of the spirit, there was a monistic implication in Tolstoy's profound veneration for the natural world.[21] When in "Berries" we read the description of children gathering wild strawberries in a wood in the early morning, with the discovery of a toddler asleep under a bush, we find something that is related, not to the philosophy of *On Life*, but to a remark that Tolstoy made in his diary on April 17, 1906: "The emotion and enthusiasm which we experience from the contemplation of nature is a recollection of the time when we were animals, trees, flowers, the earth. More exactly: it is the awareness of our unity with everything, an awareness concealed from us by time."

Albina and her husband in "What For?" were real people. Tolstoy found their story in *Siberia and Penal Servitude* by Sergei Maximov, published in three volumes in 1871. He also found there a narrative of Sirocynski's plot and the terrible punishment that followed its discovery, which he used in section 7 of "What For?" A translation of the relevant passages in Maximov's third volume forms the appendix of the present book, so that readers may see for themselves the extent of Tolstoy's indebtedness and invention. Tolstoy took the name of his Cossack from Maximov, though the original Danilo Lifanov appeared not in Albina's story but in quite a different connection.[22]

Divine and Human
and Other Stories

What For?

1

In the spring of 1830 there came to Pan Jaczewski on his ancestral estate, Rożanka, young Józef Migurski, the only son of his deceased friend. Jaczewski was a sixty-five-year-old, broad-browed, broad-shouldered, broad-chested old man, with a long white mustache on his brick-red face. He was a patriot of the time of the second partition of Poland. As a youth together with Migurski senior he had served under the banners of Kościuszko. With all the strength of his patriotic soul he hated the apocalyptic whore, as he called Catherine II, and the traitor, her vile lover Poniatowski, and believed in the restoration of the Rzeczpospolita just as he believed at night that the sun would rise again in the morning. In 1812 he commanded a regiment in the army of Napoleon, whom he adored. Napoleon's ruin grieved him, but he did not despair of the restoration of the Polish kingdom even though it would be mutilated. The opening of the Sejm in Warsaw by Alexander I revived his hope, but the Holy Alliance, the reaction throughout Europe, and Konstantin's petty tyranny postponed the realization of his cherished desire. In 1825 Jaczewski settled in the country, and from then on he lived without interruption at Rożanka, occupying his time with managing the estate, hunting, and reading newspapers and letters, by means of which he followed eagerly the political events occurring in his fatherland. He was married for a second time, to a poor, beautiful lady of the *szlachta*, but this marriage was unhappy. He did not love or respect his second wife. Feeling her to be a burden, he treated her roughly and rudely, as if punishing her for his own mistake in making this second marriage. His second wife bore no children. His first wife had left two daughters: the older, Wanda, a majestic beauty, who knew the value of her own beauty and was bored in the country, and the younger, Albina, her father's favorite, a lively, rawboned girl with curly blond hair and big, sparkling, blue eyes, which, like her father's, were set wide apart.

Albina was fifteen when Józef Migurski came. As a student Migurski had been with the Jaczewskis before, when they spent the winters at Wilno, and he had courted Wanda. Now, for the first time as a full-grown, free man he came to them in the country. Young Migurski's visit was pleasant to all the inmates of Rożanka. The old man liked Józio Migurski because he reminded him of his father, Jaczewski's friend, when they were both young, and also because he spoke with ardor and the rosiest hopes about the revolutionary ferment not only in Poland but also abroad, from where he had only just come. Pani Jaczewska liked Migurski because old Jaczewski controlled himself in front of guests and did not as usual scold her about everything. Wanda liked him because she was convinced that Migurski had come for her and intended to propose to her. She was ready to give him her consent but intended, as she said to herself, *lui tenir la dragée haute*. Albina was glad because everyone else was. Wanda was not alone in being convinced that Migurski had come with the intention of proposing to her. Everyone in the house thought so—from old Jaczewski to Ludwika the nurse—though no one said so.

It was true. Migurski had come with this intention, but after staying for a week he went away, somewhat embarrassed and downcast, without having made a proposal. Everyone was surprised at this unexpected departure, and no one, except Albina, understood its cause. Albina knew that she was the cause of this strange departure. Throughout his stay at Rożanka she noticed that Migurski was particularly excited and happy only with her. He treated her like a child, joking with her and teasing her, but with a woman's instinct she felt that in his treatment of her there was the relation not of an adult to a child, but of a man to a woman. She saw this in the loving look and tender smile with which he greeted her when she came into the room and followed her when she went out. She was not clearly aware of what this was, but his relation to her gladdened her and she tried involuntarily to do what he liked. He liked whatever she did. So it was that in his presence she did everything with particular excitement. He liked the way she ran races with a beautiful *chart* (greyhound), which jumped up at her and licked her flushed and beaming face. He liked the way she laughed on the slightest occasion with a merry, infectious, and ringing laugh. He liked the way, while continuing to laugh happily with her eyes, she put on a serious expression at a boring sermon from the *ksiądz*. He liked the way she imitated with unusual fidelity and humor now the old nurse, now a drunken neighbor, now Migurski himself, passing in a moment from the portrayal of one to the portrayal of another. Above all he liked her rapturous joy of life, which was as if she had only just learned fully the whole charm of life and hastened to enjoy it. He liked this particular joy of life of hers, but it was excited and strengthened by her knowledge that this joy of life delighted him. So it was that Albina knew why Migurski, who had come to propose to Wanda, went away without doing so. Although she would not have resolved to tell anyone about this and did not admit it clearly even to herself, she knew in the depth of her soul that he had wanted to fall in love with her sister but had fallen in love with her, Albina. Albina was very surprised at this, reckoning herself quite worthless in comparison with the intelligent, educated, and beautiful Wanda, but she could not help knowing that this was so, and could not help rejoicing at it, because she had come to love Migurski with all the strength of her soul, to love him as one can love for the first and only time in life.

2

At the end of the summer the papers brought news of the Parisian revolution. This was followed by news of imminent disorders in Warsaw. With fear and hope Jaczewski waited at every post for news of the assassination of Konstantin and the beginning of the revolution. At last in November they first received news at Rożanka of the attack on the Belvedere and of the flight of Konstantin Pavlovich, and then news that the Sejm had declared the dynasty of the Romanovs to be deprived of the Polish throne and that Chłopicki was declared dictator and the Polish people were again free. The uprising had not yet reached Rożanka, but all the inhabitants followed its course, expected it to come, and prepared for it. Old Jaczewski corresponded with an old acquaintance, one of the leaders of the uprising, received secret Jewish agents, not for economic but for revolutionary affairs, and prepared to join the uprising when the time came. Pani Jaczewska looked after her husband's material comforts, not merely as she always did, but with greater care than ever, and irritated him more and more by this very care. Wanda sent her jewelry to a friend in Warsaw, in order that the money received for it might be given to the revolutionary committee. Albina was interested only in what Migurski was doing. She knew through her father that he had joined a detachment under Dwernicki, and she tried to find out everything concerning this detachment. Migurski wrote twice: once he informed them that he had joined the army; and the second time, in the middle of February, he wrote a rapturous letter about the Poles' victory at Stoczek, where they took six Russian guns and some prisoners. "*Zwycięstwo Polaków i klęska Moskali! Wiwat!*" he wrote at the conclusion of his letter. Albina was in raptures. She examined a map, calculating where and when the Muscovites would be finally defeated, and grew pale and trembled when her father slowly unsealed some packets that arrived by post. Once her stepmother, on entering her room, found her in front of the mirror in pantaloons and a *konfederatka*. Albina was preparing to run away from home in men's clothes, so as to join the Polish army. Her stepmother told her father, who called his daughter, and concealing his sympathy and even admiration for her, he gave her a severe talking to, insisting that she put out of her head her stupid thoughts of participation in the war. "A woman has another duty: to love and comfort those who sacrifice themselves for their fatherland," he told her. Now he needed her, she was his joy and comfort, but the time would come when her husband would need her in the same way. He knew how to influence her. He hinted that he was lonely and unhappy, and he kissed her. She pressed her face against him to hide her tears, which, however, wetted the sleeve of his dressing gown, and she promised not to undertake anything without his consent.

3

Only those who have experienced what the Poles experienced after the partition of Poland and the subjection of one part of it to the power of the hated Germans, and another to the power of the still more hated Muscovites, can understand the rapture that the Poles felt in 1830 and 1831, when after previous unfortunate attempts at liberation a new hope of liberation seemed capable of being realized. But this hope did not last long. The forces were too disproportionate, and the revolution was again crushed. Again tens of thousands of Russians were driven into Poland in senseless obedience, and under the command now of Diebitsch and now of Paskevich and the supreme manager, Nicholas I, without knowing why they did so, soaking the ground with their own blood and that of their brothers, the Poles, they crushed them and returned them again to the power of weak and worthless people, who did not want either the freedom or the suppression of the Poles, but only one thing: the satisfaction of their own self-interest and childish vanity.

Warsaw was taken, and the various detachments were smashed. Hundreds and thousands of people were shot, flogged, and exiled. Among those exiled was young Migurski. His estate was confiscated, and he was assigned as a soldier to a line battalion in Uralsk.

The Jaczewskis spent the winter of 1832 in Wilno for the health of the old man, who suffered heart disease after 1831. Here a letter reached them from Migurski in a fortress. He wrote that however hard were the things that he had endured and that awaited him, he was glad that he had to suffer for his fatherland, that he did not despair of the sacred cause to which he had given part of his life and was ready to give the remainder of it, and that if a new opportunity arose tomorrow, he would act in the same way. Reading the letter aloud, the old man began to sob at this place and was long unable to continue. In the rest of the letter, which Wanda read aloud, Migurski wrote that *whatever were his plans and dreams* during his last visit, which would remain forever the brightest point in the whole of his life, he could not speak of them now, nor did he want to.

Wanda and Albina each understood the meaning of these words in her own way but did not explain to anyone how they understood them. At the end of the letter Migurski sent greetings to them all, and by the way, in the playful tone with which he had addressed Albina at the time of his visit, he addressed her in the letter, asking her if she ran just as fast, leaving *charts* behind, and if she mimicked everyone just as well. He wished the old man good health, the mother success in her household management, Wanda a worthy husband, and Albina continuation of the same joy of life.

4

Old Jaczewski's health got worse and worse, and in 1833 the whole family went abroad. Wanda met a rich Polish emigrant at Baden and married him. The old man's illness worsened rapidly, and early in 1833 he died abroad in Albina's arms. He did not allow his wife to nurse him, and until his last minute he could not forgive her for the mistake that he had made in marrying her. Pani Jaczewska returned to the country with Albina. The chief interest of Albina's life was Migurski. In her eyes he was the greatest hero and martyr, to whose service she resolved to devote her life. Even before their departure to go abroad she had begun to correspond with him, at first on her father's behalf and then by herself. Having returned to Russia after her father's death, she continued the correspondence, and when she turned eighteen she announced to her stepmother that she had resolved to go to Migurski at Uralsk, in order to marry him there. Her stepmother began to blame Migurski for egotistically wanting to alleviate his burdensome position by attracting a rich girl and making her share his misfortune. Albina got angry and declared to her stepmother that only she could ascribe such mean thoughts to a man who had sacrificed everything for his people, that, on the contrary, Migurski had refused the help she had offered him, and that she had decided irrevocably to go to him and marry him, if he only wanted to give her that happiness. Albina was of age and had money—the thirty thousand zlotys that her deceased uncle had left to his two nieces. So nothing could detain her.

In November 1833 Albina said good-bye to the servants, who saw her off with tears as she was going, as if to her death, to a distant and unknown region of barbaric Muscovy. With the devoted old nurse Ludwika, whom she was taking with her, she sat in her father's closed sleigh, which had been newly repaired for the long journey, and set out on the long journey.

5

Migurski lived not in barracks, but in his own separate quarters. Nicholas Pavlovich demanded that the Poles who were reduced to the ranks should not only bear all the hardships of a soldier's life, but also suffer all the humiliations that common soldiers were subjected to at that time. But most of the simple people who had to carry out these orders of his understood all the hardship of the degraded officers' position, and despite the danger of failure to perform his will, they did not perform it if they could avoid doing so. The commander of the battalion into which Migurski had been enlisted, a semiliterate man who had risen from the ranks, understood the position of the formerly rich, educated young man who had been deprived of everything, felt sorry for him, and respected him and granted him every kind of indulgence. Migurski could not but value the good nature of the lieutenant colonel with white whiskers on his soldier's puffy face, and to repay him he agreed to teach mathematics and French to his sons, who were preparing for military school.

Migurski's life at Uralsk, which had already dragged on for seven months, was not only monotonous, dreary, and boring, but also burdensome. Apart from the battalion commander, from whom he tried to keep away as much as possible, his only acquaintance was a Polish exile, an unpleasant, intrusive man of little education who was occupied here with commercial fishing. The chief hardship of Migurski's life was his difficulty in getting used to poverty. After the confiscation of his estate he had no means at all, and he supported himself by the sale of the golden trinkets that remained to him.

The single and great joy of his life after his exile was correspondence with Albina, of whom a sweet and poetic idea remained in his soul from the time of his visit to Rożanka and now during his banishment grew more and more beautiful. In one of her first letters she asked him, by the way, what the meaning was of the words in his former letter, "whatever were my desires and dreams." He replied that he could now confess to her that his dreams were that he would call her his wife. She replied that she loved him. He replied that it would have been better if she had not written that, because it was terrible for him to think of what could have been and was now impossible. She replied that this was not only possible, but it certainly would be. He replied that he could not accept her sacrifice, that in his present position it was impossible. Shortly after sending this letter he received notification of the remittance of two thousand zlotys. He knew by the stamp on the envelope and by the handwriting that this had been sent by Albina, and he remembered that in one of his first letters to her he had described in a joking tone the pleasure that he now felt in earning by his lessons all that he needed—money for tea, tobacco, and even books. Having put the money into another envelope, he sent it back with a letter in which he asked her not to spoil their sacred relationship with money. Everything was fine with him, he wrote, and he was quite happy knowing that he had such a friend as her. With this their correspondence ceased.

In November Migurski was at the lieutenant colonel's, giving a lesson to the boys, when they heard the sound of an approaching postal bell, and the runners of a sleigh creaked on the frozen snow and stopped at the porch. The children jumped up to see who had arrived. Migurski remained in the room, looking at the door and waiting for the children to come back, but the colonel's wife entered.

"For you, *pan*, some ladies have come and are asking for you," she said. "I suppose, from your land, like—Poles."

If Migurski had been asked whether he reckoned it possible that Albina would come to him, he would have said that it was unthinkable; but in the depth of his soul he awaited her. The blood rushed to his heart, and he ran breathlessly into the hallway. In the hallway a stout, pockmarked woman was untying a kerchief on her head. Another woman was entering the colonel's quarters. Hearing steps behind her, she looked around. From under her hood there shone the blue eyes, sparkling with the joy of life and set wide apart, of Albina, with her eyelashes covered with hoarfrost. He was dumbfounded and did not know how to welcome her, how to greet her. "Józio!" she cried, calling him by the name that her father had used and that she used to herself. She put her arms around his neck, pressed her cold, blushing face to his face, and laughed and wept.

When the colonel's good wife learned who Albina was and why she had come, she took her in and lodged her in her house until the wedding.

6

The good-natured lieutenant colonel obtained the permission of the higher authorities. A *ksiądz* was sent for from Orenburg, and the Migurskis were married. The battalion commander's wife was sponsor, one of the pupils carried an icon, and Brzozowski, the exiled Pole, was best man.

However strange it may appear, Albina loved her husband passionately without knowing him in the least. She only got to know him now. It goes without saying that in a living man of flesh and blood she found much that was so ordinary and unpoetic that it was not contained in the idea that she had borne and cultivated in her imagination; but just because this was a man of flesh and blood she also found in him much that was so simple and good that it was not included in that abstract idea. She had heard from acquaintances and friends about his bravery in the war and knew of his fortitude in bearing the loss of his fortune and freedom, and she had imagined him as a hero, always living an exalted, heroic life. In reality, with his unusual physical strength and bravery, he proved to be the simplest man, as gentle and mild as a lamb, with his good-natured jokes, with the most childlike smile on his sensual lips, surrounded by a fair, short beard and mustache—a smile that had attracted her at Rożanka—and with an inextinguishable pipe, which she found particularly hard to bear during pregnancy.

Migurski only now got to know Albina, and in Albina for the first time he got to know woman. He could not know women by the women with whom he had been acquainted before his marriage. What he found in Albina as woman in general surprised him and could have soon disappointed him about woman in general, if he had not had for Albina as Albina a particularly tender and grateful feeling. For Albina as woman in general he felt an affectionate and rather ironical condescension, but for Albina as Albina he felt not only tender love, but also admiration and consciousness of a debt too great to be repaid for her sacrifice, which had given him undeserved happiness.

The Migurskis were happy inasmuch as, directing the whole force of their love toward each other while living among strangers, they experienced the feeling of two people who have lost their way in winter and are freezing but keep each other warm. Ludwika's participation in the Migurskis' life contributed to its joy. The peevish but good-natured comic nurse, who fell in love with every man she saw, was slavishly and selflessly devoted to her *paniusia*. The Migurskis were happy with their children. A boy was born after a year, and a girl a year and a half after that. The boy was just like his mother: the same eyes and the same playfulness and grace. The girl was a healthy, beautiful little animal.

The Migurskis were unhappy because of their exile from their native land and chiefly because of the hardship of their unusually humble position. Albina especially suffered from this humiliation. He, her Józio, a hero, the ideal of a man, had to stand at attention in front of every officer, do rifle drill, go on guard, and obey orders without a murmur.

Moreover, the news that they received from Poland was very sad. Almost all their close relatives and friends had either been exiled or fled the country, losing all their property. For the Migurskis themselves no end to their situation was expected. All attempts to petition for a pardon or even for some amelioration of their condition, for promotion to the rank of an officer, were in vain. Nicholas Pavlovich held reviews, parades, and exercises, went to masquerades, flirted with masks, galloped through Russia unnecessarily from Chuguev to Novorossiisk, Petersburg and Moscow, intimidating the people and overdriving his horses, and when some brave fellow resolved to ask for alleviation of the lot of the exiled Decembrists or Poles, who were suffering as a result of the same love for their fatherland as he himself had extolled, thrusting out his chest, he would fix his metallic eyes on something and say: "Let them serve. Early." As if he knew when it would not be early and when it would be time. And all his retinue—generals, gentlemen in waiting, and their wives, eating around him—would be touched by the extraordinary sagacity and wisdom of this great man.

Nevertheless, in general in the Migurskis' life there was more happiness than unhappiness.

So they lived for five years. But suddenly an unexpected and terrible misfortune befell them. First the girl fell ill, and two days later the boy fell ill; he had a fever for three days, and without the aid of doctors (it was impossible to find one), on the fourth day he died. The girl died two days after him.

Albina did not drown herself in the Ural only because she could not imagine without horror her husband's reaction to the news of her suicide. But it was difficult for her to live. She who had always been active and busy now left all her cares to Ludwika and would sit for hours without doing anything, looking silently at whatever was under her eyes, and then she would suddenly jump up and run to her closet, where, not responding to the consolations of her husband and Ludwika, she would weep quietly, only shaking her head and asking them to go away and leave her alone. In summer she would go off to her children's grave and sit there, rending her heart with recollections of what had been and thoughts of what could have been. She was particularly tormented by the thought that the children could have survived if they had lived in a town where medical aid could have been given. "What for? What for?" she thought. "Józio and I—we don't want anything from anyone, except for him to live as he was born to and as his forefathers lived, and for me only—to live with him, love him, love my little ones, and bring them up. And suddenly they torment him, exile him, and deprive me of what is dearer than the world. Why? What for?" She put this question to people and to God, and she could not conceive the possibility of any answer.

Without an answer there was no life. Her life stopped. A poor life in exile, which she had previously been able to adorn with her feminine taste and elegance, now became unbearable not only for her, but also for Migurski, who suffered for her and did not know how to help her.

7

At this time, which was so difficult for the Migurskis, there arrived at Uralsk a Pole named Rosolowski, who had been involved in a grandiose plan of insurrection and escape, organized at the time in Siberia by the exiled *ksiądz* Sirocynski.

Rosolowski, just like Migurski and just like thousands of people punished with exile in Siberia for wanting to be what they were born to be—Poles—had been involved in that plot and had been birched for it and conscripted into the same battalion as Migurski. Rosolowski, who used to be a teacher of mathematics, was a long, thin, round-shouldered man with sunken cheeks and a frown.

On the first evening of his stay Rosolowski, sitting at tea at the Migurskis', began, quite naturally, to talk in his slow, calm bass about the plot for which he had suffered so cruelly. The plot was this: Sirocynski had organized throughout Siberia a secret society, whose aim was, with the assistance of the Poles enlisted in Cossack and line regiments, to incite the soldiers and convicts to rebellion, stir up the settlers, seize the artillery at Omsk, and set everyone free.

"Was that really possible?" Migurski asked.

"Quite possible. Everything was ready," said Rosolowski, frowning gloomily, and he slowly and calmly explained the whole plan of liberation and all the measures taken for the success of the plot and, in the event of failure, for the safety of the conspirators. Success was certain but for the treachery of two scoundrels. Sirocynski, in Rosolowski's words, was a man of genius and of great inner strength. He died as a hero and a martyr. And Rosolowski in his smooth, calm bass began to describe the details of the torture that, on the order of the authorities, he had to attend together with all those tried for this plot.

"Two battalions of soldiers stood in two ranks—a long street—and each soldier held a flexible cane of such a thickness, prescribed at the highest level, that only three could go into the muzzle of a gun. First they led Dr. Szakalski. Two soldiers led him, and those with the canes beat him on his naked back when he was level with them. I saw this only when he approached the place where I was standing. At first I heard only the roll of a drum, but then, when I began to hear the whistle of canes and the sound of blows on a body, I knew that he was approaching. I saw how the soldiers pulled him behind a gun, and he walked flinching and turning his head from side to side. Once, when they were leading him past us, I heard the Russian doctor say to the soldiers: 'Don't strike hard. Have pity.' But they struck all the same. When they led him past me the second time, he was no longer walking but they were dragging him. It was terrible to look at his back. I closed my eyes. He fell, and they carried him away. Then they led a second. Then a third, then a fourth. They all fell and were carried away—some in a dead faint, others scarcely alive—and we had to stand and watch it all. This lasted for six hours—from early morning until two o'clock in the afternoon. The last one they led was Sirocynski. I had not seen him for a long time and would not have recognized him, he had aged so. His shaven face, all in wrinkles, was pale green. His naked body was thin and yellow. His ribs protruded above his drawn-in belly. He walked just like all the others, flinching and jerking his head up at every blow, but he did not groan but loudly recited the prayer *Miserere mei Deus secundum magnam misericordiam tuam.*

"I heard it myself," Rosolowski wheezed quickly, and closing his mouth, he began to sniff.

Ludwika, who was sitting at the window, sobbed, covering her face with her kerchief.

"How can you describe it! Brutes—they're brutes!" Migurski cried, and throwing away his pipe, he jumped up from his chair and went out with quick steps into the dark bedroom. Albina sat as if turned to stone, staring into a dark corner.

8

The next day Migurski, coming home from teaching, was surprised at the sight of his wife, who, as in former times, met him with light steps and a beaming face and led him into the bedroom.

"Now, Józio, listen."

"I'm listening. What is it?"

"I thought all night about what Rosolowski told us. And I've decided: I cannot live like this, I cannot live here. I cannot! I shall die, but I will not stay here."

"What shall we do?"

"Escape."

"Escape? How?"

"I've thought it all out. Listen."

She told him the plan that she had devised the night before. The plan was this: Migurski would go out of the house in the evening and leave his overcoat on the bank of the Ural, and in the overcoat would be a letter in which he wrote that he was going to deprive himself of life. They would assume that he had drowned himself. They would look for his body; they would dispatch papers. But he would be hiding. She would hide him so well that no one would find him. It would be possible to live like that at least for a month. When everything had quieted down, they would escape.

At first her venture seemed impracticable to Migurski, but at the end of the day, when she had persuaded him with such passion and confidence, he began to agree with her. Besides, he was inclined to agree all the more because although punishment for an unsuccessful escape, the same punishment as that which Rosolowski had described, might befall him, yet success would set her free, and he saw how burdensome life here was for her after the death of their children.

Rosolowski and Ludwika were admitted into the project, and after long deliberations, changes, and corrections the plan of escape was worked out. At first they wanted to arrange it so that after Migurski had been presumed drowned, he would escape alone on foot. Albina would depart in a carriage and meet him at an appointed place. Such was the first plan. But then, when Rosolowski had recounted all the unsuccessful attempts at escape from Siberia in the last five years (in all this time only one lucky man had escaped and saved himself), Albina suggested another plan, by which Józio, hidden in the carriage, would travel with her and Ludwika as far as Saratov. At Saratov he would walk in disguise along the bank of the Volga and at an appointed place board a boat that she would hire at Saratov and in which he would sail together with Albina and Ludwika down the Volga to Astrakhan and across the Caspian Sea to Persia. This plan was approved by everyone, including the chief organizer, Rosolowski, but the problem arose of finding such space in a carriage as would not attract the attention of the authorities but would nevertheless be able to accommodate a man. When Albina, after a trip to the children's grave, told Rosolowski how painful it would be for her to leave the children's remains in a strange land, he thought and said:

"Ask the authorities for permission to take the children's coffins with you. They will let you."

"No, no! I don't want that!" said Albina.

"Ask. Everything depends on it. We won't take the coffins, but we'll make a big box for them and in the box we'll put Józef."

At first Albina rejected this proposal, it was so unpleasant to her to connect deceit with the memory of her children, but when Migurski cheerfully approved of this project, she agreed to it.

So the final plan that they worked out was this: Migurski would do everything necessary to convince the authorities that he had drowned himself. When his death was acknowledged, Albina would submit an application for permission, after her husband's death, to return to her native land and to take her children's remains with her. When this permission was granted, they would make it look as if the grave had been opened and the coffins taken out, but the coffins would stay in place, and instead of the children's coffins Migurski would be put in a box prepared for this purpose. They would put the box into a tarantass and so travel to Saratov. From Saratov they would board a boat. In the boat Józio would come out of the box, and they would sail to the Caspian Sea. Then Persia or Turkey and—freedom.

9

First of all the Migurskis bought a tarantass under the pretext of sending Ludwika back to her own country. Then began the installation in the tarantass of a box in which it would be possible to lie without suffocating, though in a cramped position, and from which it would be possible to get out quickly without being noticed and get into it again. Albina, Rosolowski, and Migurski together devised and fitted the box. Rosolowski's help was especially important, since he was a good joiner. The box was made so that when it was fixed in place behind the body of the tarantass, it fitted tightly against the body, and the side that was against the body came off, so that by pulling out the side, a man could lie partly in the box and partly on the floor of the tarantass. Further, airholes were drilled in the box, and it had to be covered with matting on its top and sides and tied with ropes. It was possible to get into it and out of it through the tarantass, in which a seat was made.

When the tarantass and the box were ready, but before her husband had disappeared, Albina, in order to prepare the authorities, went to the colonel and announced that her husband had fallen into melancholy and attempted suicide and that she feared for him and asked for his leave of absence for a while. Her talent for dramatic art stood her in good stead. The anxiety and fear for her husband that she expressed were so natural that the colonel was touched and promised to do all he could. After this Migurski composed the letter that was to be found in the pocket of his overcoat on the bank of the Ural, and on the appointed day, in the evening, he went to the Ural, waited for darkness, put his clothes on the bank, including the overcoat with the letter, and secretly returned home. A place for him had been prepared in the garret, which was kept locked. Albina sent Ludwika to the colonel at night to inform him that her husband, who had left home twenty hours before, had not returned. In the morning they brought her her husband's letter, and she took it to the colonel with an expression of intense despair and in tears.

Within a week Albina submitted an application to depart for her native land. The grief that Migurska expressed struck all who saw her. Everyone pitied the unhappy mother and wife. When her departure was permitted, she submitted another application—for leave to exhume her children's corpses and take them with her. The authorities marveled at this sentimentality but permitted it.

The day after receipt of this permission Rosolowski, Albina, and Ludwika went in the evening to the cemetery, to the children's grave, in a hired wagon with the box into which the children's coffins were to be put. Albina prayed on her knees at the grave and quickly stood up and, turning to Rosolowski with a frown, said:

"Do what is necessary. I cannot," and stepped aside.

Rosolowski and Ludwika moved the gravestone and dug the upper parts of the grave with a spade so that the grave looked as if it had been dug up. When it was all done, they called Albina and returned home with the box filled with soil.

The appointed day of departure came. Rosolowski was pleased with the success of the enterprise, which was almost completed. Ludwika baked biscuits and patties for the journey and, repeating her favorite saying, "*Jak mamę kocham,*" said that her heart was breaking with fear and joy. Migurski was pleased to be released from the garret, in which he had sat for more than a month, and pleased above all with Albina's animation and joy of life. It was as if she had forgotten all her former grief and all the danger. Running to him in the garret, she beamed with rapturous joy, as she had done when a girl.

At three o'clock in the morning a Cossack came to escort them and a Cossack coachman brought a troika of horses. Albina and Ludwika with a lapdog sat in the tarantass on cushions, covered with a rug. The Cossack and the coachman sat on the driver's seat. Migurski, dressed in peasant's clothes, lay in the body of the tarantass.

They drove out of the town, and the good troika drew the tarantass along a road beaten smooth like stone, across the unending, unplowed steppe, overgrown with last year's silvery feather-grass.

10

Albina's heart stood still in her breast with hope and rapture. Wishing to share her feelings, she now and then with a slight smile at Ludwika nodded now toward the broad back of the Cossack sitting on the driver's seat and now toward the floor of the tarantass. Ludwika looked steadily in front of her with a significant expression and only pursed her lips a little. It was a clear day. On all sides stretched the boundless, uninhabited steppe, shining with silvery feather-grass in the slanting rays of the morning sun. Only now on this and now on that side of the hard road, on which the quick, unshod hooves of the Bashkir horses resounded as if on asphalt, could be seen little mounds of soil heaped up by susliks. A little animal sat on its hindquarters on guard, whistled shrilly to give notice of danger, and hid in its burrow. They rarely met other travelers: a string of Cossacks' carts with wheat or mounted Bashkirs, with whom the Cossack exchanged words in fluent Tatar. At every station the horses were fresh and well fed, and the fifty copecks that Albina gave for vodka made the coachmen drive, as they said, like couriers—at a gallop the whole way.

At the first station, when the previous coachman had led his horses away but the new one had not yet brought fresh horses and the Cossack had gone into the yard, Albina leaned over and asked her husband how he felt and whether he needed anything.

"Fine, comfortable. I don't need anything. I can easily lie here for two days."

Toward evening they came to the large village of Dergachi. So that her husband could stretch his legs and refresh himself, Albina stopped not at the post station, but at the inn, and at once giving money to the Cossack, she sent him to buy her eggs and milk. The tarantass stood under the penthouse; it was dark in the yard; and having put Ludwika where she could watch for the Cossack, Albina let her husband out and fed him, and he got back into his secret place before the Cossack's return. They sent for horses again and traveled farther. Albina felt more and more elation and could not restrain her rapture and gaiety. She had no one to talk to except Ludwika, the Cossack, and Trezorka, and she amused herself with them.

Ludwika, who, despite her plainness, in any relation she had with a man immediately suspected that he was attracted to her, now suspected this in her relation with the muscular, good-natured Ural Cossack with unusually clear and kindly blue eyes, who was escorting them and who was particularly agreeable to both women with his simplicity and good-natured tenderness. Besides Trezorka, whom Albina scolded, not allowing him to sniff under the seat, she now amused herself with Ludwika and her comic coquetry with the Cossack, who did not suspect the intentions attributed to him and smiled good-naturedly at everything they said to him. Albina, excited by the danger, by the success of the venture that was beginning to be realized, and by the wonderful weather and the air of tne steppe, had a feeling of childlike rapture and gaiety that she had not experienced for a long time. Migurski heard her merry talk, and in spite of the physical discomfort of his place of hiding (he was particularly hot and tormented by thirst), forgetting about himself, he rejoiced in her joy.

Toward evening on the second day something became visible

in the mist. This was Saratov and the Volga. The Cossack, with his eyes accustomed to the steppe, saw the Volga and the masts of ships and pointed them out to Ludwika, who said that she saw them, too. But Albina could not make anything out. She said loudly on purpose so that her husband would hear:

"Saratov, the Volga." As if she were talking to Trezorka, Albina told her husband everything that she saw.

11

Without entering Saratov, Albina stopped on the left bank of the Volga, at the Pokrovskaya settlement, opposite the town. Here she hoped to have time in the course of the night to talk with her husband and even to get him out of the box. But the Cossack did not leave the tarantass the whole short spring night, but sat beside it in an empty wagon parked under the penthouse. Ludwika, on Albina's order, sat in the tarantass and, being fully convinced that the Cossack did not leave the tarantass for her sake, winked, laughed, and hid her pockmarked face in her kerchief. Albina no longer saw anything amusing in this but grew more and more anxious, not understanding why the Cossack constantly hung around the tarantass.

Several times in the short May night that merged with twilight, Albina walked out of her room in the inn past the stinking gallery onto the back porch. The Cossack was never asleep but, dangling his legs, sat on the empty wagon parked beside the tarantass. Only before dawn, when the cocks had woken up and were crowing from yard to yard, did Albina, coming down, find time to talk with her husband. The Cossack was snoring, sprawling in the wagon. She cautiously approached the tarantass and pushed the box.

"Józio!" There was no answer. "Józio, Józio!" She spoke more loudly from fright.

"What is it, darling?" Migurski said in a sleepy voice from the box.

"Why didn't you answer?"

"I was asleep," he said, and she knew by the sound of his voice that he was smiling. "What then, get out?" he asked.

"You can't. The Cossack's here." Having said this, she looked at the Cossack, sleeping in the wagon.

Strange to say, although the Cossack was snoring, his eyes, his kindly blue eyes, were open. He was looking at her, and only when she met his gaze did he close his eyes.

"Did that just seem so to me or was he really not asleep?" Albina asked herself. "It seemed so, most likely," she thought and addressed her husband again.

"Be patient a little longer," she said. "Do you want to eat?"

"No. I want to smoke."

Albina looked at the Cossack again. He was asleep. "Yes, it just seemed so to me," she thought.

"I'm going to the governor now."

"Well, good luck!"

Having taken some clothes out of a trunk, Albina went to her room to get dressed.

When she had changed into her best widow's dress, Albina crossed the Volga. On the quay she took a cab and went to the governor's. The governor received her. The pretty Polish widow, smiling sweetly and speaking perfect French, delighted the would-be young but actually old governor. He granted her everything and asked her to come again the next day to obtain from him an order addressed to the mayor of Tsaritsyn. Rejoicing at the success of her petition and at the effect of her attractiveness, which she saw in the governor's manner, Albina, happy and full of hopes, returned downhill in a carriage along an unpaved street to the pier. The sun had risen above the woods and played with its slanting beams on the rippling water of the vast flood. To right and left on the hill apple trees drenched with odorous blossoms could be seen, like white clouds. A forest of masts could be seen by the bank, and sails showed white on the flood as it played in the sun and rippled in the breeze. Talking with a cabman on the pier, Albina asked if it was possible to hire a boat to go to Astrakhan, and dozens of noisy, jolly boatmen offered her their services and their boats. She made an agreement with one of them, whom she liked more than the others, and went to look at his boat, standing by the pier in a narrow space between other boats. The boat was fitted with a short mast with a sail, so that it could go by the wind. There were oars in case of a calm and two strong, jolly barge haulers, who also worked as rowers, sitting in the boat in the sun. The jolly, good-natured pilot advised Albina not to leave the tarantass but to take the wheels off and put it on the boat. "Once it's fixed, you can sit comfortably. If God gives fine weather, we'll get to Astrakhan in five days."

Albina made a bargain with the boatman and told him to go to the Loginov inn at the Pokrovskaya settlement, to look at the tarantass and receive a deposit. Everything had turned out better than she had expected. In the most rapturously happy state of mind Albina crossed the Volga and, having settled her account with the cabman, directed her steps toward the inn.

12

The Cossack Danilo Lifanov was from Streletskii Umet on Obshchii Syrt. He was thirty-four years old and was serving the last month of his term of duty as a Cossack. In his family there was an old man, a ninety-year-old grandfather, who still remembered Pugachev, two brothers, the daughter-in-law of the older brother, who had been sent to hard labor in Siberia for being an Old Believer, Danilo's wife, two daughters, and two sons. His father had been killed in the war with the French. He was the oldest in the house. In his yard he had sixteen horses and two teams of oxen, and fifteen *sotenniks* of his free land were plowed and sown with wheat. Danilo had served at Orenburg and Kazan and was now finishing his term. He adhered firmly to the Old Belief, did not smoke, did not drink, and did not eat from the same dish as those who were not Old Believers, and he adhered to his oath of allegiance just as strictly. In all his affairs he was slow, steady, and reliable, and when acting on the authorities' instructions, he gave the task his full attention, not neglecting it for a minute, until he had performed it all as he understood it. Now he had been ordered to escort two Polish women with some coffins to Saratov, so that they wouldn't come to any harm on the way but would travel peacefully without getting up to any pranks, and at Saratov to hand them over to the authorities in a proper fashion. So he had brought them to Saratov with a wee dog and with their coffins and all. The women were quiet and endearing, though they were Poles, and didn't do anything wrong. But here at the Pokrovskaya settlement, toward evening, as he was passing the tarantass, he saw the little dog jump up into the tarantass and there begin to yelp and wag its tail, and someone's voice came from under the seat. One of the Polish women, the old one, seeing the dog in the tarantass, was frightened at something, grabbed the dog, and took it away.

"Something's up," the Cossack thought, and began to watch. When the young Polish woman came out at night to the tarantass, he pretended to be asleep and clearly heard a man's voice coming from the box. Early in the morning he went to the police and reported that the Polish women entrusted to him were not traveling innocently but instead of corpses were carrying a live man in the box.

When Albina approached the inn in her rapturously happy state of mind, and in the conviction that everything was now completed and they would be free in a few days' time, she was surprised to see by the gate a dandified couple with a trace horse in harness and two Cossacks. A crowd had gathered at the gate, looking into the yard.

She was so full of hope and energy that it did not enter her head that that couple and the crowd of people had anything to do with her. She went into the yard, and just when she looked under the penthouse where her tarantass was parked, she saw that the people were crowding around her tarantass, and at the same moment she heard Trezorka's desperate bark. The most terrible thing that could have happened had happened. In front of the tarantass, gleaming in his clean uniform with buttons that shone in the sun, shoulder straps, and polished boots, there stood a portly man with black whiskers, who was saying something in a loud, raucous, and commanding voice. In front of him, between two soldiers, stood her Józio in peasant's clothes and with hay in his disheveled hair. As if bewildered by what was occurring around him, he raised and lowered his powerful shoulders. Trezorka, not knowing that he was the cause of the whole calamity, bristled up and barked at the chief of police uselessly and angrily. On seeing Albina, Migurski started and wanted to go to her, but the soldiers held him back.

"Never mind, Albina, never mind!" Migurski said, smiling his gentle smile.

"Ah, here is the lady herself," said the chief of police. "Please come here. Where are your babies' coffins? Ah?" he said, winking at Migurski.

Albina did not answer, but clasping her bosom, with her mouth open, she looked at her husband in horror.

As happens in the moments before death and generally in decisive moments in life, in an instant she experienced a mass of feelings and thoughts but at the same time did not yet understand, did not believe her own misfortune. Her first feeling had long been familiar to her—a feeling of insulted pride at the sight of her hero-husband humiliated in front of these rough, wild people who now held him in their power. "How dare they hold *him*, the best of all people, in their power?" Another feeling, which seized her at the same time as this, was an awareness of the misfortune that had occurred. This awareness of misfortune called up the memory of the greatest calamity of her life, the death of her children. And at once arose the question What for? What were her children taken away for? The question What were her children taken away for? called up the question What was her beloved husband, the best of men, perishing for, being tormented for? And now she recalled what shameful punishment awaited him, and that she, she alone, was to blame.

"What is he to you? Is he your husband?" the chief of police repeated.

"What for, what for?" she screamed, and going off into hysterical laughter, she fell onto the box, which had now been taken down and was lying beside the tarantass. Ludwika went to her, shaking from head to foot with sobs and with her face flooded with tears.

"*Panienka,* darling *panienka! Jak Boga kocham,* nothing will come of it, nothing," she said, senselessly passing her hands over her.

They put manacles on Migurski and led him out of the yard. On seeing this, Albina ran after him.

"Forgive, forgive me!" she said. "It's all my fault. I alone am to blame."

"They will inquire who is to blame. You will hear about it," the chief of police said, and pushed her aside with his arm.

They led Migurski to the ferry, and Albina went after him, without knowing why she did so, and did not listen to Ludwika talking to her.

All this time the Cossack Danilo Lifanov stood by a wheel of the tarantass and looked gloomily now at the chief of police, now at Albina, and now at his feet.

When Migurski had been led away, Trezorka was left alone and, wagging his tail, began to fawn upon Danilo. He had got used to him during the journey. The Cossack suddenly turned away from the tarantass, tore off his cap, flung it to the ground with all his might, spurned Trezorka with his foot, and went into the eating house. In the eating house he ordered vodka and drank day and night; he drank everything that he had on him, and only on the next night, when he woke up in a ditch, did he stop thinking about the question that tormented him: Had he done well in informing the authorities of the Polish woman's husband in the box?

Migurski was tried and sentenced for desertion to running the gauntlet of a thousand lashes. His relatives and Wanda, who had connections in Petersburg, managed to obtain mitigation of his punishment, and he was sent into perpetual exile in Siberia. Albina followed him.

Nicholas Pavlovich was glad that he had crushed the hydra of revolution not only in Poland, but throughout Europe, and was proud of the fact that he had not broken the principles of the Russian autocracy but for the good of the Russian people kept Poland in the power of Russia. Men wearing stars and gilded uniforms praised him so highly for this that he sincerely believed he was a great man and that his life was a great blessing for mankind and particularly for the Russian people, to whose corruption and stupefaction all his forces were unconsciously directed.

Divine and Human

1

It was in the 1870s in Russia, at the height of the struggle between the revolutionaries and the government.

The governor-general of the southern region, a sturdy German with a drooping mustache, a cold look, and an expressionless face, wearing a military coat with a white cross at the neck, sat in his study one evening at a table with four candles in green shades, looking over and signing papers that the first secretary had left with him. "Adjutant-General So-and-So," he inscribed with a long flourish, laying each paper aside.

Among the papers was a death sentence by hanging, passed on Anatolii Svetlogub, a student at the University of Novorossiya, for taking part in a plot that had as its aim the overthrow of the existing government. Frowning more than usual, the general signed this paper, too. With his white, well-manicured fingers, wrinkled with age and soap, he accurately lined up the edges of the pages and laid them aside. The next paper was about fixing the costs of the transportation of provisions. He was reading this paper attentively, wondering whether the calculations were correct or not, when he suddenly remembered his conversation with his assistant about Svetlogub. The general did not think that the discovery of dynamite in Svetlogub's rooms proved his criminal intention. The assistant stressed that besides the dynamite there was a lot of evidence to prove that Svetlogub was the chief of the gang. Remembering this, the general pondered, and under his coat with padding in the breast and lapels as stiff as cardboard his heart beat unsteadily, and he began to breathe so heavily that the big white cross, his pride and joy, stirred on his chest. He could still call back the first secretary and if not cancel the sentence, then postpone it.

"Call him back? Or not?"

His heart beat more unsteadily. He rang. A courier came in with quick, silent steps.

"Has Ivan Matveevich left?"

"No, Your Excellency. He has gone into the office."

The general's heart now stopped and now gave rapid thumps. He remembered the warning from the doctor who had listened to his heart a day or two before.

"Above all," the doctor had said, "as soon as you feel that it is your heart, stop work, amuse yourself. Worst of all is agitation. Don't on any account allow it."

"Do you want me to call him?"

"No, there's no need," said the general. "Yes," he said to himself, "indecision is the worst kind of agitation. It's signed—and finished. *Ein jeder macht sich sein Bett und muss d'rauf schlafen,*" he repeated his favorite saying to himself. "This does not concern me. I am executor of the highest will and should stand above such considerations," he added, knitting his brows so as to summon the cruelty that was not in his heart.

He remembered his last meeting with the emperor and how the emperor, putting on a stern expression and fixing his glassy gaze on him, had said: "I rely on you. As you did not spare yourself in the war, you will act just as resolutely in the struggle with the Reds. You do not let yourself be deceived or frightened. Good-bye!" The emperor embraced him and offered him his shoulder to kiss. The general remembered this and also how he had answered the emperor: "My one desire is to give my life in the service of my emperor and fatherland."

Remembering the feeling of servile tenderness that he had experienced at the idea of his selfless devotion to his emperor, he drove away the thought that had disturbed him for a moment, signed the remaining papers, and rang again.

"Is tea served?" he asked.

"They are just serving it, Your Excellency."

"Good, you may go."

The general sighed deeply and, rubbing the place where his heart was, went with heavy steps into the large, empty hall and across the freshly polished parquet floor into the drawing room, from which he heard voices.

The general's wife had guests, the governor with his wife, an old princess, who was a great patriot, and a guards officer, engaged to the general's last unmarried daughter.

The general's wife, wizened, with a cold expression and thin lips, sitting at a low table, on which stood a tea set with a silver teapot on a ring, was talking in a tone of feigned sadness to a stout, would-be youthful lady, the governor's wife, about her concern for her husband's health.

"Every day new reports reveal conspiracies and all sorts of horrible things. . . . And all this falls to Basil; he has to cope with it all."

"Ah, don't talk about it!" said the princess. "*Je deviens féroce quand je pense à cette maudite engeance.*"

"Yes, yes, it's terrible. Can you believe it? He works twelve hours a day, and with his weak heart. I'm just afraid . . ."

She did not finish, seeing her husband enter.

"Yes, you must hear him. Barbini is a wonderful tenor," she

said, smiling pleasantly at the governor's wife. She referred to a singer who had recently arrived, as naturally as if they had been talking only about him.

The general's daughter, a plump, pretty girl, was sitting with her fiancé in a far corner of the drawing room, behind a little Chinese screen. She stood up and with her fiancé approached her father.

"Well, we haven't seen each other today!" said the general, kissing his daughter and shaking hands with her fiancé.

Having greeted the guests, the general sat at the table and talked with the governor about the latest news.

"No, no, don't talk about those things. It's forbidden!" The general's wife interrupted the governor as he was speaking. "Here's Kopyev. He will tell us something amusing. Good evening, Kopyev!"

Kopyev, well known for his gaiety and wit, indeed told the latest anecdote, which made everyone laugh.

2

"No, it can't be, it can't, it can't! Let me go!" cried Svetlogub's mother with a scream, struggling to break from the arms of a high school teacher, a colleague of her son's, and a doctor, who were trying to restrain her.

Svetlogub's mother was a comely, middle-aged woman, with curls that were touched with gray and with little starlike wrinkles around her eyes. The teacher, Svetlogub's colleague, having learned that the death sentence had been signed, wanted to prepare her carefully for the terrible news, but as soon as he began to speak about her son, she guessed by the tone of his voice and by his timid look that what she dreaded had occurred.

This took place in a small apartment in the best hotel in the town.

"Why are you holding me? Let me go!" she cried, trying to tear herself away from the doctor, an old friend of the family, who held her with one hand by her thin elbow and with the other placed a bottle of drops on an oval table in front of the divan. She was glad that they held her, because she felt that she had to do something, but what, she did not know and was afraid of herself.

"Calm down. Here, drink this tincture of valerian," said the doctor, giving her a muddy liquid in a glass.

She suddenly quieted down and almost bent double, dropping her head on her sunken breast, and closing her eyes, she collapsed on the divan.

She remembered how three months before her son had said good-bye to her with a mysterious and sorrowful face. Then she recalled him as an eight-year-old boy in a little velvet jacket, with bare legs and with his fair hair in long, curly ringlets.

"Him, him, this same boy . . . they are going to do this to him!"

She jumped up, pushed away the table, and tore herself from the doctor's arms. Reaching the door, she fell into an armchair.

"They say there's a God! What sort of God is he if he allows this! Devil take him, this God!" she cried, now sobbing, now going off into fits of hysterical laughter. "They are going to hang him, hang him, who abandoned everything, his whole career, gave up his whole fortune to others, to the people, gave it all up," she said. Previously she had always reproached her son for this, but now she represented to herself the merit of his self-denial. "Him, him, they are going to do this to him! And you say there's a God!" she shrieked.

"I don't say anything. I only ask you to drink these drops."

"I don't want anything. Ha-ha-ha!" She laughed and sobbed, drunk with her own despair.

By nightfall she was so exhausted that she could no longer speak or weep but only looked in front of her with a fixed, insane stare. The doctor sprinkled her with morphine, and she fell asleep.

Waking up, after a dreamless sleep, was still more horrible. Most horrible of all was that people could be so cruel, not only those horrible generals with shaven cheeks and those gendarmes, but everyone, everyone: the servant girl, with a calm face coming to do the room, and the people in the next apartment, who greeted one another cheerfully and laughed about something, as though nothing had happened.

3

Svetlogub sat in solitary confinement for a second month, and during this time he suffered much.

From childhood Svetlogub had unconsciously felt the injustice of his exceptional position as one of the rich, and although he tried to suppress this awareness in himself, yet often on meeting people in need, and sometimes simply on particularly pleasant and joyful occasions, he felt ashamed before those people—peasants, old men, women, children—who were born, grew up, and died not only not knowing all those pleasures that he enjoyed without valuing them, but who did not even get any relief from strenuous labor and from need. When he left the university, in order to free himself from this consciousness of his own injustice, he started a school of his own in a village—a model school—a consumers' cooperative shop, and a shelter for unfortunate old men and women. But, strange to say, while he was occupied with these things, he felt much more ashamed in front of the people than when he had supper with his friends or bought an expensive saddle horse. He felt that all this was not right, and worse than not right: there was in it something bad, morally unclean.

In one of these moods of disappointment with his rural activities, he went to Kiev, where he met one of his closest companions from the university. Three years after this meeting this companion was shot in the ditch at the Kiev fortress.

This companion, a passionate and enthusiastic man with great gifts, persuaded Svetlogub to join a society whose aim was to enlighten the people, to evoke in them a consciousness of their rights, and to form among them organized circles striving for liberation from the power of the landowners and the government. Conversations with this man and his friends as it were brought into clear consciousness everything that Svetlogub had until then dimly perceived. Now he understood what he had to do. Without breaking off with his new comrades, he went back to the village and began some altogether new activities there. He became a schoolteacher himself, arranged classes for adults, read them books and pamphlets, and explained the peasants' position to them; besides this, he published illegal popular books and pamphlets and spent all he could, without depriving his mother, on the establishment of such centers in other villages.

From the first steps he took with these new activities Svetlogub met two unexpected obstacles. One was that most of the people were not only indifferent to his propaganda, but looked upon him almost with contempt. (Only exceptional personages and often those of doubtful morality understood and sympathized with him.) The other obstacle had to do with the government. His school was closed, he and his associates were searched, and their books and papers were confiscated.

Svetlogub paid little attention to the first obstacle, the indifference of the people, since he was too perturbed by the second, the government's senseless and insulting oppression. His comrades in his activities and in other places had the same experience, and a feeling of anger with the government, which was kindled among them, reached the point at which the greater part of this circle decided to struggle against the government by force.

The chief of this circle was a certain Mezhenetskii, a man whom everyone considered to have unflinching strength of will, to argue with irrefutable logic, and to be wholly committed to the cause of revolution.

Svetlogub came under the influence of this man, and with the same energy with which he had previously worked among the people he devoted himself to terrorism. The very danger of this activity attracted him more than anything. He said to himself, "Victory or martyrdom, and if martyrdom, then martyrdom is victory, but only in the future." And the fire lit within him, far from dying out in the course of his seven years of revolutionary activities, flared up more and more, fed by his love and respect for the people with whom he associated.

He did not attach any importance to the fact that he devoted almost all his fortune to this cause (a fortune he had inherited from his father), nor did he attach any importance to the difficul- ties and the indigence that he often endured. Only one thing grieved him: this was the grief that he inflicted on his mother and her ward, a girl who lived with his mother and was in love with him.

An unpleasant comrade, whom he did not like much, a terror- ist wanted by the police, had lately asked Svetlogub to hide some dynamite. Svetlogub agreed to do so without hesitation precisely because he did not like this comrade, and on the following day his flat was searched and the dynamite discovered. He refused to answer any of the questions put to him about how and wherefrom he had obtained the dynamite.

So the martyrdom that he had expected began for him. Lately, when so many of his friends were executed, imprisoned, or exiled, and when so many women suffered, Svetlogub had almost desired martyrdom. In the first minutes of his arrest and interrogation he felt a peculiar excitement, almost joy.

He had this feeling when they stripped and searched him and when they led him into prison and locked an iron door on him. But when a day passed and another and a third, and a week passed and another and a third in his dirty, damp cell, which was infested with insects, and he remained in solitude and in involuntary idleness, interrupted only by communications by tapping with his fellow prisoners, who always passed on bad and depressing news, and by occasional interrogations with cold and hostile people, who tried to extract from him some incrimination of his comrades, then his moral strength together with his physical weakened steadily, and he only felt dejected, longing, as he said to himself, for some end to this tormenting position. His dejection increased the more he doubted his own strength. In the second month of his incarceration he began to imagine himself revealing the whole truth, only in order to be set free. He was horrified at his own weakness, but not finding his former strength, he hated and despised himself and became still more dejected.

The most terrible thing was that in his incarceration he began to regret the youthful energy and joy that he had sacrificed so easily while he was free, and which now seemed so attractive that he repented of what he had considered to be good, repented sometimes of all of his activities. Thoughts came to him about how happily and well he could live in freedom—in the country or abroad, among loved and loving friends. To marry her, or perhaps another, and live with her a simple, joyful, and radiant life.

4

On one of these tormentingly monotonous days in the second month of Svetlogub's imprisonment, the inspector on his usual round gave him a little book with a golden cross on its brown cover, saying that the governor's wife had visited the prison and left some copies of the Gospels for distribution among the inmates. Svetlogub thanked him and smiled slightly, putting the book on the small table that was screwed into the wall.

When the inspector had gone, Svetlogub and his neighbors by means of tapping discussed his visit, agreeing that he had not said anything new but only brought Gospels.

After dinner Svetlogub opened the little book with its pages stuck together by the damp and began to read. He had never before read the Gospels as a book. All he knew about them was what the divinity teacher had gone through in high school and what the priests and deacons read in church in a singsong.

"Chapter one. The book of the generation of Jesus Christ, the son of David, the son of Abraham. . . . Isaac begat Jacob; and Jacob begat Judas . . . ," he read. "And Zorobabel begat Abiud," he continued to read. All this was what he had expected: some confused and quite unnecessary nonsense. If he had not been in prison, he could not have read one page, but here he continued to read for the sake of reading. "Like Gogol's Petrushka," he thought to himself. He read the first chapter on the virgin birth and the prophecy that they would call the son's name Emmanuel, which meant "God with us." "What's the point of this prophecy?" he thought as he continued to read. He read the second chapter— on the moving star—and the third—on John feeding on locusts— and the fourth—on some devil offering Christ gymnastic exercise from a roof. All this seemed so uninteresting to him that in spite of the boredom of the prison he already wanted to close the book and begin his usual evening occupation—catching fleas in the shirt he took off—when he suddenly remembered that in the examination in the fifth form at high school he had forgotten one of the beatitudes, and the pink-faced, curly-headed parson had suddenly got angry and given him a failing grade. Not being able to recall what this one was, he read the beatitudes. "Blessed are they which are persecuted for righteousness' sake: for theirs is the kingdom of heaven," he read. "This may apply to us," he thought. "Blessed are ye, when men shall revile you, and persecute you. . . . Rejoice, and be exceeding glad . . . for so persecuted they the prophets which were before you. Ye are the salt of the earth: but if the salt have lost his savor, wherewith shall it be salted? It is thenceforth good for nothing, but to be cast out, and to be trodden under foot of men."

"This applies to us completely," he thought, and continued to read. Having read the whole of the fifth chapter, he pondered: "Do not be angry, do not lust, endure evil, love your enemies."

"Yes, if everyone lived like that," he thought, "a revolution would not be needed." Reading further, he entered more and more deeply into the meaning of those parts of the book that were quite comprehensible. The further he read, the more he came to think that in this book something particularly important was said—important, simple, and affecting, such as he had never heard before yet had, as it were, long been familiar with.

"Then said Jesus unto his disciples, If any man come after me, let him deny himself, and take up his cross, and follow me. For whosoever will save his life shall lose it: and whosoever will lose his life for my sake shall find it. For what is a man profited, if he shall gain the whole world and lose his own soul?"

"Yes, yes, this is it!" he suddenly cried out with tears in his eyes. "I wanted to do just this. Yes, I wanted just this: to give my soul; not save it, but give it. This is joy, this is life. I did a lot for people, for their praise," he thought, "not the praise of the crowd, but for the good opinion of those whom I respected and loved—Natasha, Dmitrii Shelomov—and then I had doubts, uneasiness. It was right for me only when I did what my soul demanded, when I wanted to give myself, to give up everything. . . ."

From that day Svetlogub spent a large part of his time reading and considering what was said in that book. This reading aroused in him not only a tender state of feeling, which lifted him out of the conditions in which he suffered, but also such mental labor as he had never before been conscious of. He wondered why people, all people, did not live as commanded in that book. "To live so is good, not for one, but for all. Only live so, and there will not be any sorrow or any indigence; there will only be blessedness. If only this could end, if only I could be free again," he thought sometimes. "They will let me out someday or send me off to hard labor. It's all the same; one can live so anywhere. And I shall live so. One can and must live so; not to live so is madness."

5

On one of those days when Svetlogub was in such a joyful and excited state of feeling, the inspector entered his cell at an unusual time and asked him if he was all right and if he wanted anything. Svetlogub was surprised, not understanding what this change meant, and asked for cigarettes, expecting a refusal. But the inspector said that he would send some straight away; and indeed a guard brought him a packet of cigarettes and some matches.

"Someone must have interceded for me," Svetlogub thought, and having lit a cigarette, he began walking up and down his cell, considering the meaning of this change.

On the next day he was taken to court. In the courtroom, where he had already been several times, they did not start interrogating him. But one of the judges, without looking at him, rose from his chair, and when the others had stood up, holding a piece of paper in his hands, he began to read in a loud and strangely expressionless voice.

Svetlogub listened and looked at the faces of the judges. None of them looked at him, but they all listened with significant and doleful expressions.

It was said in the paper that it had been proved that Anatolii Svetlogub had participated in revolutionary activities that had as their aim the overthrow of the existing government in the more near or distant future, and that therefore he was sentenced to the deprivation of all his rights and to the penalty of death by hanging.

Svetlogub heard and understood the meaning of the words pronounced by the officer. He noticed the absurdity of the words "in the more near or distant future" and of the deprivation of the rights of a man sentenced to death, but he altogether failed to understand the meaning that what was read had for him.

Only long after he had been told that he could go and he had gone out onto the street with a gendarme did he begin to understand what had been declared to him.

"Something's not right, not right. . . . This is some nonsense. It can't be," he said to himself, sitting in the coach that carried him back to prison.

He felt within himself such strength of life that he could not imagine death, could not combine his consciousness of his self with death, with the absence of self.

Back in his cell, Svetlogub sat on the bed and, closing his eyes, tried to imagine vividly what was awaiting him, but he could not do so in any way. In no way could he imagine that he would not be; he could not imagine that people could want to kill him.

"Me, young, good, happy, loved by so many people," he thought, and he remembered his mother's, Natasha's, and his friends' love for him, "they are going to kill me, hang me! Who will do this? Why? And then what will be when I am not? It can't be," he said to himself.

The inspector came in. Svetlogub did not hear him.

"Who's that? Who are you?" he said, not recognizing the inspector. "Ah yes, it's you. When is this going to be?" he asked.

"I'm not in a position to know," replied the inspector, and after standing in silence for several seconds, he suddenly said in a tender and ingratiating voice, "Our parson would like . . . the bungler . . . would like to see you. . . ."

"I don't need him, don't need him. I don't need anything! Get out!" Svetlogub cried.

"Shouldn't you write to anyone? You may," said the inspector.

"Yes, yes, send me the things. I'll write."

The inspector went out.

"So it'll be in the morning," Svetlogub thought. "They always do it like this. Tomorrow morning I shall be no more. . . . No, it can't be. It's a dream."

But the guard came in, the real guard whom he was familiar with, bringing two pens, an inkpot, a packet of notepaper, and pale blue envelopes, and he placed a stool in front of the table. All this was real and not a dream.

"I shouldn't think about it, shouldn't think. Yes, yes, write. I'll write to Mama," he thought. He sat on the stool and immediately began to write.

"My dear darling!" he wrote, and burst into tears. "Forgive me, forgive me for all the sorrow that I have caused you. Whether I was mistaken or not, I could not have acted differently. I ask you one thing: Forgive me." "I've written this before," he thought. "Well, it's all the same. Now there isn't time to rewrite it." "Do not grieve for me," he wrote further. "A little sooner or later—isn't it all the same? I am not afraid and do not repent of what I have done. I could not have acted differently. Only forgive me. Do not be angry with them—neither those with whom I worked nor those who execute me. Neither of them could have acted differently. Forgive them, for they know not what they do. I dare not repeat these words about myself, but they are in my soul and uplift and soothe me. Forgive! I kiss your dear, wrinkled, old hands." Two tears one after the other dropped onto the paper and ran on it. "I am weeping, though not from grief or fear, but from a tender feeling at the most solemn moment of my life, and because I love you. Do not blame my friends, but love them. Especially Prokhorov, just because he was the cause of my death. It is so joyful to love someone who is not guilty but who can be blamed or hated. To love such a man—your enemy—is such happiness! Tell Natasha that her love was my comfort and joy. I did not understand this clearly, but I recognized it in the depth of my soul. It was easier for me to live, knowing that she existed and that she loved me. Well, I have said everything. Good-bye!"

He reread the letter, and when he came to Prokhorov's name it suddenly occurred to him that the authorities could read the letter, that they certainly would read it, and this would destroy Prokhorov.

"My God, what have I done!" he suddenly cried, and after tearing the letter into long strips, he began to burn them assiduously at the lamp.

He had sat down to write in despair, but now he felt calm, almost joyful.

He took another sheet and at once began to write. One after another his thoughts crowded in his head.

"Dear, darling Mama!" he wrote, and again his eyes grew dim with tears. He had to wipe them with the sleeve of his jacket, to see what he wrote. "How I failed to know myself, to know the whole strength of my love for you and the gratitude that always lived in my heart! Now I know and feel that love and gratitude, and when I remember our disagreements and the unkind words that I spoke to you, I am sorry and ashamed, and it is almost incomprehensible. Forgive me and remember only the good, if there was any in me.

"I am not afraid of death. To tell the truth, I do not understand it, do not believe in it. You see, if there is death, annihilation, then isn't it all the same whether I die thirty years or thirty minutes sooner or later? If there is no death, then it is altogether the same, sooner or later."

"But I am philosophizing," he thought. "I must say what was in the other letter, something good at the end. Yes." "Do not blame my friends but love them and especially him who was the involuntary cause of my death. Kiss Natasha for me and tell her that I always loved her."

He folded the letter, sealed it, and sat on the bed, putting his arms on his knees and gulping down his tears.

He still did not believe that he had to die. Several times, again putting the question to himself whether he was not asleep, he tried in vain to wake up. This thought led him to another, whether the whole of life in this world was not a dream, the awakening from which would be death. "If so, then is not the consciousness of life in this world only an awakening from the dream of a previous life, the details of which I do not remember? So life here is not a beginning, but only a new form of life. I shall die and pass into a new form." This thought pleased him; but when he wanted to lean on it, he felt that this thought, and indeed every thought, no matter what, was unable to give tranquillity in the face of death. At last he got tired of thinking. His brain worked no more. He closed his eyes and sat for a long time, without thinking.

"Well then? What will be?" again he reflected. "Nothing? No, not nothing. But what?"

It suddenly struck him quite clearly that for a living human being there was not and could not be an answer to these questions.

"So why do I ask myself about it? Why? Yes, why? You don't have to ask; you have to live as I did just now when I wrote that letter. Look, we were all condemned long ago, always, and yet we live. We live well, joyfully, when . . . we love. Yes, when we love. When I wrote that letter I loved, and it was well with me. That's how you have to live. And you can live anywhere and at any time, free, in prison, today, tomorrow, and to the very end."

He wanted now to talk with someone affectionately, lovingly. He knocked on the door, and when the sentry looked at him he asked him the time and whether he would soon be relieved, but the sentry did not reply to him at all. Then he asked him to call the inspector. The inspector came, asking what he wanted.

"I've written a letter to my mother; give it to her, please," he said, tears coming into his eyes at the recollection of his mother.

The inspector took the letter and, promising to have it delivered, wanted to go, but Svetlogub stopped him.

"Listen. You are good. Why do you serve in this distressing position?" he said, touching him affectionately on the sleeve.

The inspector smiled with unnatural pity and, lowering his eyes, said:

"One has to live."

"Quit this position. Look, you can always get a job. You're so good. Perhaps I could—"

The inspector suddenly sobbed, turned abruptly, and went out, slamming the door.

The inspector's agitation moved Svetlogub all the more, and holding back tears of joy, he began to walk from wall to wall, not experiencing any fear now, only a tender state of feeling that raised him above the world.

That very question, what would become of him after death, which he had tried so hard to answer but in vain, seemed to be solved for him, not with any positive, rational answer, but with the consciousness of the true life that was in him.

He remembered the words of the Gospel: "Verily, verily I say unto you, Except a corn of wheat fall into the ground and die, it abideth alone: but if it die, it bringeth forth much fruit." "Now I shall fall into the ground. Yes, verily, verily," he thought.

"Go to sleep," he suddenly thought, "so as not to weaken then." He lay on the bed, closed his eyes, and immediately fell asleep.

He woke up at six o'clock in the morning, wholly under the influence of a radiant and happy dream. He dreamed that with a little fair-haired girl he climbed up spreading trees that were loaded with ripe black cherries and gathered them in a big brass basin. The cherries miss the basin and fall onto the ground, and some strange animals like cats catch the cherries, toss them up, and catch them again. Looking at this, the girl laughs with such infectious merriment that Svetlogub too laughs happily in his sleep, without knowing why. Suddenly the brass basin slips from the girl's hands. He wants to catch it but is not quick enough, and the basin, knocking against the branches, falls onto the ground with a clatter. He wakes up, smiling and listening to the prolonged clatter of the basin. This clatter is the sound of the iron bolts being opened in the corridor. Steps are heard along the corridor, and the crash of arms. He suddenly remembers everything. "Ah, if only I could sleep again!" he thinks, but it is now impossible to sleep. The steps have reached his door. He hears how a key looks for the lock and how the door creaks as it is opened.

There have entered an officer of the gendarmes, the inspector, and an escort. "Death? Well, what then? I shall go. Yes, it is well. All is well," Svetlogub thinks, feeling the return of that state of solemn tenderness that he was in yesterday.

6

In the same prison in which Svetlogub was held, an old man was held, a priestless schismatic who doubted his leaders and sought the true faith. He denied not only the Nikonian Church, but also the government from the time of Peter, whom he considered to be the Antichrist. He called the imperial power a "tobacco power" and boldly stated what he thought, exposing priests and officials. For this he was tried and confined to jail and transferred from one prison to another. That he was not free but in prison, that inspectors swore at him, that they put him in irons, that the other prisoners jeered at him, that they all, like the authorities, renounced God and swore at one another and in every possible way defiled the divine image in themselves—none of this concerned him, for he had seen all this everywhere in the world when he had been free. All this, he knew, proceeded from the fact that people had lost the true faith and had all gone astray, like blind puppies from their mother. But meanwhile he knew what the true faith was. He knew this because he felt this faith in his heart. And he sought this faith everywhere. Above all he hoped to find it in the Revelation of St. John.

"He that is unjust, let him be unjust still: and he which is filthy, let him be filthy still: and he that is righteous, let him be righteous still: and he that is holy, let him be holy still. And, behold, I come quickly; and my reward is with me, to give every man according as his work shall be." He constantly read this mysterious book, and every minute he awaited him who was coming, and who would not only give to every man according to his works, but also reveal the whole divine truth to people.

On the morning of Svetlogub's execution the schismatic heard the drums, and having climbed up to a window, he saw through the bars how a chariot was brought out and how a youth with radiant eyes and curly hair came out of the prison and, with a smile, got onto the chariot. In the youth's small white hand there was a book. The youth pressed the book to his heart—the schismatic knew that it was the Gospels—and nodding to the prisoners at the windows and smiling, he exchanged glances with them. The horses started, and with the youth sitting on it as radiant as an angel, the chariot, surrounded by guards and rumbling over the stones, went out through the gates.

The schismatic climbed down from the window, sat on his bed, and pondered. "He knew the truth," he thought. "The servants of Antichrist give him the rope so he can't reveal it to anyone."

7

It was an overcast autumnal morning. The sun was not to be seen. A warm, humid wind blew from the sea.

The fresh air, the sight of houses, of the town, of horses, and of people looking at him—all this diverted Svetlogub. Sitting on the chariot's bench, with his back to the coachman, he looked involuntarily into the faces of the soldiers escorting him and of the townsfolk whom they met.

It was an early hour of the morning. The streets through which he was driven were almost empty, and they met only workers. Bricklayers splashed with lime and wearing aprons walked hurriedly toward him but stopped and turned back when they were level with the chariot. One of them said something, waving his arm, and they all turned around and went back to their own business. Wagoners carrying clanking strips of iron turned their big horses to give way to the chariot but stopped and looked at Svetlogub with puzzled curiosity. One of them took off his cap and crossed himself. A cook in a white apron and cap, with a basket in her hand, came out of a gate, but on seeing the chariot, she quickly turned into a courtyard and ran out again with another woman, and they both, without pausing for breath, followed the chariot with wide-open eyes as long as they could see it. An unshaven, gray-haired man, dressed in rags, expressed evident disapproval to the yard keeper with energetic gestures, pointing to Svetlogub. Two boys caught up with the chariot at a trot, and with their heads turned, not looking in front of them, they walked beside it along the pavement. One, the older, went with quick steps; the other, a little boy without a cap, holding on to the older and looking timidly at the chariot, could hardly keep in step with him but stumbled along on his short little legs. Meeting his eyes, Svetlogub nodded to him. This gesture from the dreadful man being carried on the chariot so confused the boy that he stared with open mouth and was going to cry. Then Svetlogub, kissing his hand, smiled affectionately at him, and the boy suddenly and unexpectedly responded with a sweet, kind smile.

Throughout this journey the consciousness of what awaited him did not disturb Svetlogub's solemn and tranquil state of mind.

Only when the chariot reached the gallows, and he was taken from it and saw the posts with a cross-beam and a rope swinging from it gently in the wind, did he feel as it were a physical blow on his heart. He suddenly felt sick. But this did not last long. Around the scaffold he saw black ranks of soldiers with arms. In front of the soldiers went officers. As soon as they began to take him from the chariot, there resounded the unexpected crash of a drumroll, which made him wince. Behind the ranks of soldiers he saw the carriages of ladies and gentlemen, who had evidently come to watch the spectacle. The sight of all this in the first minute astonished Svetlogub, but once he recollected what he had been before he went to prison, he felt sorry that those people did not know what he now knew. "But they will learn. I shall die, but the truth will not die. They will know. And like everyone—not I, but they all could be and will be happy."

They led him onto the scaffold, and an officer followed him. The drums fell silent, and in an unnatural voice, which sounded particularly weak in the midst of a broad field and after the crash of the drums, the officer read the stupid death sentence that had been read to Svetlogub in court, about the deprivation of the rights of a man whom they were killing and about the near and distant future. "Why, why are they doing all this?" he thought. "What a pity that they don't yet know and that I can no longer communicate it all to them! But they will learn. They will all learn."

A lean priest with long, thin hair came up to Svetlogub. He wore a violet cassock, with a small gilded cross on his breast and a large silver cross that he held in his weak, white, stringy, thin hand, protruding from his black velvet cuff.

"Merciful Lord," he began, transferring the cross from his left hand to his right and presenting it to Svetlogub.

Svetlogub flinched and moved away. He almost said something unkind to the priest, who spoke of mercy while taking part in the deed that was being accomplished, but remembering the words of the Gospel—"they know not what they do"—he made an effort and spoke shyly:

"Excuse me, I don't need this. Please, pardon me, but really I don't need it. Thank you."

He held out his hand to the priest, who transferred the cross to his left hand, pressed Svetlogub's hand, trying not to look him in the face, and went down from the scaffold. The drums crashed again, drowning all other sounds.

After the priest, a middle-aged man approached Svetlogub with quick steps, shaking the boards of the scaffold. He had sloping shoulders and muscular arms and wore a coat over a Russian shirt. This man, after a quick look at Svetlogub, came right up to him and, pouring over him an unpleasant smell of wine and sweat, seized him by the wrists with tenacious fingers, and squeezing his wrists so that they hurt, he turned them behind his back and tied them tightly. Having tied his arms, the hangman paused for a minute, as if considering, and looking now at Svetlogub, now at some things he had brought with him and put on the scaffold, and now at the rope hanging from the cross-beam. Having considered what he had to do, he went to the rope, did something with it, and pushed Svetlogub forward toward the rope and the edge of the scaffold.

Just as at the announcement of the death sentence Svetlogub had not been able to understand the whole meaning of what was declared to him, so now he could not grasp the whole meaning of the coming moment and looked at the hangman with wonder, as he hastily, dexterously, and attentively performed his terrible task. The hangman's face was the ordinary face of a Russian working-man, not evil, but concentrated, such as belongs to people who try to perform a necessary and complicated task as precisely as possible.

"Move here a bit farther . . . ," said the hangman in a hoarse voice, pushing him toward the gallows. Svetlogub moved.

"Lord, help, have mercy on me!" he said.

Svetlogub did not believe in God and often used to laugh at people who did. Even now he did not believe in God, because not only to put such a belief into words, but to comprehend him in thought was impossible. But what he understood now by him to whom he appealed was something he knew to be the most real of everything he knew. He knew that this appeal was necessary and important. He knew this because this appeal at once calmed and strengthened him.

He moved toward the gallows, and involuntarily glancing over the ranks of soldiers and motley spectators, he thought again: "Why, why are they doing this?" He pitied them and himself, and tears came into his eyes.

"Don't you pity me?" he said, catching the sharp gray eyes of the hangman.

The hangman paused for a moment. His face suddenly became angry.

"You! Talking!" he muttered, and quickly stooped to the floor, where his coat and some linen lay. Then, clasping Svetlogub from behind with a dexterous movement of both hands, he threw a linen sack over his head and hastily pulled it halfway down his back and chest.

"Into thy hands I commend my spirit," Svetlogub remembered the words of the Gospel.

His spirit was not opposed to death, but his strong young body did not accept it, did not submit, and wanted to struggle.

He wanted to scream, to break away, but at the same moment he felt a jerk, a loss of support, the physical horror of suffocation, a noise in his head, and the disappearance of everything.

Svetlogub's body hung from the rope, swinging. His shoulders rose and sank twice.

After waiting two minutes, the hangman, with a gloomy frown, put his hands on the shoulders of the corpse and pulled it down with a strong movement. All movement of the corpse ceased, except for the slow swinging of a doll hanging in a sack, with the head thrust forward unnaturally and the legs stretched out in prisoner's stockings.

Descending from the scaffold, the hangman informed the officer in charge that the corpse could be taken down from the noose and buried.

In an hour the corpse was taken down from the gallows and carried away to an unconsecrated burial ground.

The hangman had performed what he wanted and had undertaken to perform. But this had not been easy. Svetlogub's words "Don't you pity me?" did not go out of his head. He was a murderer, a convict, and the title of hangman gave him relative freedom and luxury of life, but from this day onward he refused to perform the duty that he had taken upon himself, and in the same week he drank not only all the money that he had received for the execution, but also all his relatively expensive clothes, and eventually he was confined to a punishment cell, and from the punishment cell he was transferred to a hospital.

8

One of the leaders of the terrorist party of revolutionaries, Ignatii Mezhenetskii, the same who had enticed Svetlogub into terrorist activities, was sent from the province where he had been arrested to Petersburg. In the same prison was the old schismatic who had seen Svetlogub being taken to execution. They were sending him to Siberia. He still wondered how and where he might discover the true faith, and he sometimes remembered that radiant youth who had smiled joyfully when going to his death.

Having learned that in the same prison with himself there was a comrade of that youth's, a man who shared his faith, the schismatic was glad and entreated a guard to take him to Svetlogub's friend.

In spite of all the strictness of the prison discipline, Mezhenetskii did not cease to communicate with people of his party and waited every day for news of the mining that he had devised and invented for the blowing up of the czar's train. Now, remembering some details that he had omitted, he was devising a means of transmitting them to his accomplices. When the guard came into his cell and told him quietly and cautiously that one of the prisoners wanted to see him, he was glad, hoping that this meeting would give him an opportunity to communicate with his party.

"Who is he?" he asked.

"A peasant."

"What does he want?"

"He wants to talk about faith."

Mezhenetskii smiled. "Well, send him in," he said. "Those schismatics hate the government, too. Perhaps he will be useful," he thought.

The guard went away, and after a few minutes, opening the door, he let into the cell a short, wizened old man who had thick hair, a thin goatee beard touched with gray, and kindly but tired blue eyes.

"What do you want?" Mezhenetskii asked.

The old man glanced up at him and, hastily lowering his eyes, he held out his small, energetic, wizened hand.

"What do you want?" Mezhenetskii repeated.

"A word with you."

"What word?"

"About faith."

"What faith?"

"They say that you are of the same faith as that youth that the servants of Antichrist gave the rope to at Odessa."

"What youth?"

"They gave it to him at Odessa in the autumn."

"Svetlogub, I suppose?"

"Yes, him. Was he a friend of yours?" At every question the old man looked searchingly into Mezhenetskii's face with his kindly eyes and immediately lowered them again.

"Yes, he was close to me."

"And of the same faith?"

"Probably the same," said Mezhenetskii, smiling.

"My word with you is about that."

"What do you want, exactly?"

"To know your faith."

"Our faith . . . Well, sit down," said Mezhenetskii, shrugging. "Our faith is this. We believe that there are men who have taken power and torment and deceive the people, and that one must not spare oneself but struggle with those men, so as to deliver from them the people whom they exploit," he said by force of habit. "Torment," he corrected himself. "They must be destroyed. They kill, and they must be killed until they come to their senses."

The old schismatic sighed without raising his eyes.

"Our faith is not to spare oneself, but to overthrow the despotic government and establish one that is free, elective, and popular."

The old man sighed heavily, stood up, straightened the skirt of his coat, got down on his knees, and lay at Mezhenetskii's feet, knocking his forehead on the dirty floorboards.

"Why are you bowing?"

"Do not deceive me. Reveal what your faith is," said the old man without getting up or raising his head.

"I have said what our faith is. Stand up, or I won't speak."

The old man got up.

"Was that the faith of that youth?" he said, standing in front of Mezhenetskii and now and then looking him in the face with his kindly eyes and immediately lowering them again.

"It was just that, and for that they hanged him. They bring me now to the Peter-Paul for the same faith."

The old man bowed from the waist and silently went out of the cell.

"No, that was not the faith of that youth," he thought. "That youth knew the true faith, but this one either boasted that he had the same faith or doesn't want to reveal it. . . . Well, I shall keep trying. Both here and in Siberia. God is everywhere, people are everywhere. Stand on the road to ask the road," the old man thought, again taking his New Testament, which opened by itself at the Revelation, and having put on his spectacles, he sat by the window and began to read.

9

Seven years passed. Mezhenetskii served solitary confinement in the Peter-Paul fortress and was sent to hard labor.

He endured much during those seven years, but the direction of his thoughts did not change, nor did his energy weaken. When under interrogation, before his confinement in the fortress, he surprised his questioners and judges with his firmness and contemptuous attitude toward those people who had him in their power. In the depth of his soul he suffered because he had been caught and could not finish the work that he had begun, but he did not show this. As soon as he came into contact with people, the energy of his anger arose. He did not reply to the questions that were put to him, and spoke only when he had a chance to wound his interrogators—an officer of the gendarmes and the public procurator.

When they said the usual words to him—"You can alleviate your condition by a frank confession"—he smiled contemptuously and after a silence replied:

"If you intend by benefit or fear to make me betray my comrades, you judge me by yourselves. Do you really think that in doing the deed for which you are trying me I did not prepare myself for the worst? So you cannot surprise me with anything or frighten me. You can do with me what you want, but I shall not speak."

It was pleasant for him to see how they looked at each other in confusion.

When, in the Peter-Paul fortress, they put him in a small, damp cell, with dark glass in a high window, he understood that this was not for months, but for years, and he was filled with horror. The well-contrived dead silence was horrible, and so was his consciousness that he was not alone, but that here, behind these impenetrable walls, were prisoners like him, sentenced to ten or twenty years, wasting away, hanging themselves, going mad, or dying slowly of consumption. Here were women and men, and friends, perhaps. . . . "Years will pass, and you too will go mad, hang yourself, or die, and they won't know about you," he thought.

Anger rose in his soul at all people, but especially at those who were the cause of his confinement. This anger demanded the presence of objects of anger; it demanded movement, noise. But here the dead silence, the soft steps of taciturn people, who did not answer questions, the sounds of doors being opened and closed, food at regular hours, the attendance of taciturn people, and through the dim glass light from the rising sun, darkness and the same silence, the same soft steps, and the same sounds. Like this today, tomorrow . . . His anger, not finding any outlet, ate away his heart.

He tried making a noise, but they did not answer him, and his noise only provoked again the same soft steps and smooth voice of a man who threatened him with a punishment cell.

The only time of rest and relief was the time of sleep. But then waking up was horrible. He always dreamed that he was free and for the most part carried away by such things as he considered to be inconsistent with revolutionary activities. Now he was playing some strange violin, now he was courting girls, now boating, now hunting, now for some strange scientific discovery he was awarded a doctorate at a foreign university and made a speech of thanks at a dinner. These dreams were so vivid, while his actual condition was so dull and monotonous, that in his memory they seemed almost real.

The hard thing about his dreams was only that for the most part he awoke at the moment when what he strove for or desired was just about to be accomplished. At a sudden jolt of his heart his joyful situation disappeared entirely; there remained a tormenting, unsatisfied desire, and again this gray wall with damp stains, lit by a small lamp, and under his body the hard bed with a hay mattress flattened down on one side.

Sleep was the best time. But the longer his confinement lasted, the less he slept. He awaited and desired sleep as the greatest happiness, and the more he desired it, the more it was driven away. He had only to ask himself the question "Am I falling asleep?" and his drowsiness passed entirely away.

Running or jumping about his cage did not help. From strenuous movement the only result was weakness and still greater agitation of the nerves, followed by a headache in the darkness. He had only to close his eyes, and against a dark background marked with sparkles ugly faces began to appear, shaggy haired, balding, big mouthed, wry mouthed, one more frightful than another. The faces grimaced with the most horrible grimaces. Then they began to appear before his open eyes, and not only faces but whole figures began to speak and dance. It grew terrible, he jumped up, beat his head against the wall, and shouted. The aperture in the door opened.

"You are not supposed to shout," said a calm, smooth voice.

"Call the inspector!" Mezhenetskii shouted.

There was no answer, and the aperture closed.

Such despair seized Mezhenetskii that he wanted only one thing—death.

Once when in such a state he decided to deprive himself of life. In the cell there was an air vent, to which it was possible to attach a rope with a noose so that, standing on the bed, he could hang himself. But there wasn't a rope. He began to tear the bedsheet into narrow strips, but these were insufficient. Then he decided to starve himself and did not eat for two days, but on the third day he weakened, and the hallucinations returned in an attack of particular force. When food was brought to him, he was lying unconscious on the floor with his eyes open.

A doctor came, put him on the bed, and gave him bromide and morphine. He fell asleep.

When he awoke the next day, the doctor was standing over him and shaking his head. Suddenly Mezhenetskii was seized with a thrill of anger, such as used to be familiar to him, but which he had not felt for a long time.

"Aren't you ashamed to serve here?" he said to the doctor while the latter, with head bent, was taking his pulse. "Why do you treat me, to torment me again? It's just the same as attending a flogging and allowing the operation to be repeated."

"Be so kind as to lie on your back," said the unruffled doctor, without looking at him but taking an instrument for auscultation out of a side pocket.

"They healed the wounds, to complete the total of five thousand lashes. Go to the devil, to the devil!" he suddenly shouted, throwing his legs off the bed. "Clear off! I shall die without you."

"This is bad, young man. We have our answers to rudeness."

"Go to the devil, to the devil!"

Mezhenetskii was so dreadful that the doctor left in a hurry.

10

Whether it was because he had taken drugs, or because he had endured his crisis, or because the outburst of anger at the doctor had cured him, Mezhenetskii took himself in hand and began quite a different life.

"They cannot and will not keep me here forever," he thought. "They'll release me sometime. Perhaps—most probably—the regime will change (our people continue their work), and therefore I must take care of myself, so as to go out strong and healthy and to be in a fit condition to continue the work."

For a long time he considered the best way to live to achieve this end, and he decided on this: He went to bed at nine o'clock and made himself lie there, whether he slept or not, until five in the morning. At five o'clock he got up, washed and tidied himself, did gymnastics, and then, as he said to himself, he went to work. In his imagination he walked through Petersburg, from Nevskii to Nadezhdinskaya, trying to picture everything that he could encounter on such an excursion: signboards, houses, policemen, carriages, and pedestrians. At Nadezhdinskaya he entered the house of an acquaintance and collaborator of his, and there, together with some other comrades who had arrived, they planned their next undertaking. There were debate and argument. Mezhenetskii spoke both for himself and for the others. Sometimes he spoke so loudly that the sentry at the aperture told him off, but Mezhenetskii did not pay him any attention and continued his imaginary day in Petersburg. Having spent two hours at his friend's, he returned home and had dinner, first in imagination and then in fact when they brought him dinner. He always ate in moderation. Then he sat at home, in imagination, and studied history, mathematics, and sometimes, on Sundays, literature. The study of history consisted of choosing a period and nation and recalling facts and chronology. The study of mathematics consisted of doing calculations and geometrical problems in his head. (He particularly liked this study.) On Sundays he recalled works of Pushkin, Gogol, and Shakespeare and told stories.

In the evening he made a little excursion, in his imagination having facetious, merry, and sometimes serious conversations with his comrades, both men and women. Some of these conversations had occurred previously, others were newly made up. This lasted until nighttime. Before going to bed, he actually took two thousand steps for exercise in his cage, and when he lay down he usually fell asleep.

The next day it was the same. Sometimes he traveled south and, stirring up the people, began an uprising and together with the people drove out the landowners and divided the land among the peasants. He imagined all this, however, not suddenly but gradually, with every detail. In his imagination the revolutionary party triumphed everywhere, and the government, its power weakened, was compelled to convene a council. The czar's family and all the oppressors of the people disappeared, a republic was established, and Mezhenetskii was elected president. Sometimes he reached this point too quickly, and then he began again from the beginning and attained the end by other means.

So he lived for a year, for two, three years, sometimes departing from this strict order of life, but for the most part keeping to it. By directing his imagination, he freed himself from the involuntary hallucinations. Only now and then did he have attacks of insomnia and visions of ugly faces, and then, looking at the air vent, he considered how to attach a rope, make a noose, and hang himself. But these attacks did not last long. He overcame them.

So he lived for almost seven years. When his term of confinement was finished and he was taken away to hard labor, he was quite fresh and healthy and in full possession of his inner strength.

As a particularly important criminal, he was taken alone and not allowed to communicate with others. Only in Krasnoyarsk prison did he for the first time succeed in making contact with other political offenders, who were also exiled to hard labor. There were six of them, two women and four men. They were young people of a new frame of mind, not known to Mezhenetskii. They were the revolutionaries of the next generation, his successors, and therefore they particularly interested him. Mezhenetskii expected to see in them people following in his footsteps and therefore bound to have a high esteem of everything that had been done by their predecessors, particularly Mezhenetskii. He was ready to treat them affectionately and condescendingly. But to his unpleasant surprise these young people not only did not consider him to be their predecessor and teacher, but treated him as it were condescendingly, disregarding or excusing his antiquated views. In the opinion of these new revolutionaries, everything that Mezhenetskii and his friends had done, all the attempts to stir up the peasants and, chiefly, terror, and all the assassinations—of the governor Kropotkin, Mezentsov, and even Alexander II—all this was a series of mistakes. All this had led only to reaction, which was triumphant under Alexander III and turned society backward, almost to serfdom. The way to liberate the people, in the opinion of the new revolutionaries, was altogether different.

In the course of two days and almost two nights the dispute between Mezhenetskii and his new acquaintances did not cease. In particular their leader, Roman, as they called him just by his first name, tormented Mezhenetskii with his unshakable confidence in his own rightness and his condescending and even derisive dismissal of all the past activities of Mezhenetskii and his comrades.

According to Roman, the people were a rude throng or "cattle," and nothing could be done with them as long as they remained at the stage of development they were now at. Every attempt to raise the Russian rural population was just like trying to set fire to stone or ice. The people had to be educated, they had to be trained to solidarity, and this could be achieved only by large-scale industrialization and the consequent growth of a socialist organization of the people. The land, far from being needed by the people, made them conservative and servile, not only among us, but also in Europe. Roman quoted from memory the opinions of authorities and statistical figures. The people had to be freed from the land, and the sooner this was done, the better. The more they worked in factories, and the more capitalists took possession of the land and oppressed the people, the better. Despotism and especially capitalism could be destroyed only by the solidarity of the people, and this solidarity could be attained only by unions, workers' corporations; and this was possible only when the masses ceased to be landholders and became proletarians.

Mezhenetskii argued and got angry. One of the women particularly annoyed him, a good-looking, long-haired brunette with very bright eyes, who, sitting by the window as if not taking a direct part in the conversation, put in a word now and then in support of Roman's reasoning or only laughed contemptuously at Mezhenetskii's words.

"Is it really possible to turn all the agricultural people into industrial?" said Mezhenetskii.

"Why not?" Roman retorted. "It's a general economic law."

"How do we know it's a general law?" said Mezhenetskii.

"Read Kautsky," the brunette put in with a contemptuous smile.

"Even if we admit," said Mezhenetskii, "(though I don't admit it) that the people will become a proletariat, why do you think that this will take the form that you have predetermined for it?"

"Because this prediction is scientifically based," replied the brunette, turning from the window.

When they talked about the kind of activity that was necessary for the attainment of their object, the disagreement became even greater. Roman and his friends insisted that they had to train an army of workers, help to turn the peasants into proletarians, and carry out socialist propaganda among the workers, and that, far from struggling openly with the government, they should use it for the attainment of their own ends. Mezhenetskii said that they had to struggle directly with the government, terrorize it, and that the government was both stronger and more cunning than they were. "You will not deceive the government, but they will deceive you. We propagandized the people and struggled with the government."

"And how much you achieved!" said the brunette ironically.

"Yes, I think that a direct struggle with the government is an unjustified waste of effort," said Roman.

"The first of March a waste of effort!" cried Mezhenetskii. "We sacrificed ourselves, our lives, but you sit quietly at home, enjoying life, and you only preach."

"We don't enjoy life very much," Roman said quietly, looking at his comrades, and he laughed triumphantly with a laugh that was not infectious, but loud, distinct, and self-confident.

The brunette, shaking her head, smiled contemptuously.

"We don't enjoy life very much," said Roman. "But if we are here, we are obliged to the reaction, and the reaction is the work precisely of the first of March."

Mezhenetskii was silent. He felt that he was choking with anger and went out into the corridor.

Trying to calm down, Mezhenetskii began to walk up and down the corridor. The doors of the cells were open until the evening roll call. He was approached by a tall, fair prisoner, who looked good-natured despite his half-shaven head.

"A prisoner in our cell saw Your Honor. 'Call him to me,' he says."

"What prisoner?"

"Tobacco Power. That's his nickname. A little old man, one of the schismatics. 'Call that man to me,' he says. Your Honor, that is."

"Where is he?"

"Here, in our cell. 'Call that gentleman,' he says."

Mezhenetskii went with the prisoner into a small cell with plank beds, on which other prisoners were sitting or lying.

On bare boards on the edge of a bed and under a gray coat lay that same old schismatic who had come to Mezhenetskii seven years ago to ask about Svetlogub. His pale face was all shriveled and wrinkled; his hair was just as thick as before, but his thin beard was now quite gray and was sticking up. His blue eyes were kindly and attentive. He lay on his back and was obviously in a fever; there was an unhealthy flush on his cheeks.

Mezhenetskii went up to him.

"What do you want?" he asked.

The old man raised himself with difficulty onto an elbow and held out a small, wizened, trembling hand. Preparing to speak, he swayed and began to breathe heavily. Struggling for breath, he said softly:

"You did not reveal it to me then. God be with you! I reveal it to all."

"What do you reveal?"

"About the Lamb . . . about the Lamb I reveal. . . . That youth was with the Lamb. It is said: 'The Lamb shall overcome them'—overcome all—'. . . and they that are with him are . . . chosen, and faithful.'"

"I do not understand," said Mezhenetskii.

"Understand in spirit. The czars take their province from the Beast. But the Lamb shall overcome."

"What czars?" said Mezhenetskii.

"'And there are seven czars: five are fallen, and one is and the other is not yet come'—has not come, that is—'and when he cometh, he must continue a short space.' That is, his end will come. . . . Understand?"

Mezhenetskii shook his head, thinking that the old man was raving and his words were meaningless. The other prisoners, his companions in the cell, thought so, too. The shaven prisoner who had called Mezhenetskii came up to him and, nudging him gently to attract his attention, winked at the old man.

"He's always chattering, chattering, is our Tobacco Power," he said. "But what about, he doesn't know himself."

Looking at the old man, Mezhenetskii and his companions in the cell thought so, too. But the old man knew quite well what he was saying, and what he was saying had a clear and profound meaning for him. The meaning was that the reign of evil would not last much longer, that the Lamb was overcoming all by goodness and humility, and that the Lamb would wipe away every tear, and there would not be any weeping or disease or death. He felt that this was already happening, happening in the whole world, because it was happening in his soul as it was enlightened by his nearness to death.

"Surely I come quickly. Amen. Even so, come, Lord Jesus," he said, and smiled significantly but, as it seemed to Mezhenetskii, insanely.

"There he is, a representative of the people," thought Mezhenet-skii as he left the old man. "He's the best of them. What darkness! They say"—he referred to Roman and his friends—"with people like him it is impossible to do anything."

At one time Mezhenetskii had done his revolutionary work among the people and knew all the "inertness," as he called it, of the Russian peasant. He had met soldiers both in the service and retired and knew their obtuse belief in the oath of allegiance, in the necessity of obedience, and the impossibility of influencing them by reason. He knew all this but had never drawn from this knowledge the conclusion that inevitably followed from it. Conversation with the new revolutionaries disturbed and annoyed him.

"They say that everything that we did, that Khalturin, Kibal-chich, and Perovskaya did, was quite useless and even harmful, that this provoked the reaction of Alexander the Third, and that thanks to them the people are convinced that all revolutionary activities come from the landowners, who killed the czar because he had taken away their serfs. What rubbish! What incomprehension and what impudence to think that!" he said to himself as he continued to pace the corridor.

The doors of all the cells were shut, except for the one that held the new revolutionaries. As he approached it, Mezhenetskii heard the laughter of the brunette he hated and Roman's firm, pompous voice. They were obviously talking about him. Mezhenetskii stopped to listen. Roman was speaking:

"Because they did not understand the laws of economics, they were not aware of what they were doing. A great part here was . . ."

Mezhenetskii could not and did not want to hear what the great part here was doing. He did not have to know. Just the tone of that man's voice showed the complete contempt these people felt for him, for Mezhenetskii, a hero of the revolution, who had lost twelve years of his life for the sake of this cause.

There arose such terrible anger in his soul as he had never felt before, anger at everyone, at everything, at all this senseless world in which people could live only like animals, such as that old man with his Lamb and these half-bestial hangmen and jailers and these insolent, self-confident, stillborn doctrinaires.

The guard on duty came in and led the political women away to the women's quarters. Mezhenetskii went to the far end of the corridor so as not to meet them. On his return the guard locked the door of the new politicals and ordered Mezhenetskii to go to his cell. He obeyed mechanically but asked the guard not to lock his door.

On returning to his cell, Mezhenetskii lay on the bed with his face to the wall.

"Have I really wasted all my efforts, spent my energy, strength of will, and genius, all for nothing?" (He never reckoned that anyone was above him in mental qualities.) He remembered that not long before, while on the way to Siberia, he had received a letter from Svetlogub's mother, reproaching him in a stupid, woman's manner, as he thought, for having destroyed her son by enticing him into the terrorist party. When he received the letter, he only smiled contemptuously. What could that stupid woman understand about the aims that he and Svetlogub had set themselves? But now, recalling the letter and Svetlogub's sweet, trusting, and ardent personality, he thought first about him and then about himself. Was all his life really a mistake? He closed his eyes and wanted to go to sleep, but suddenly he felt with horror the return of the condition that he had been in during his first month in the Peter-Paul fortress. Again pain in the darkness, again ugly faces, big mouthed, hairy, horrible, against a dark background with little stars, and again figures appearing before his open eyes. What was new was that some criminal in gray trousers and with a shaven head swung over him. Again, by association of ideas, he began to look for an air vent to which it might be possible to attach a rope.

Intolerable anger, demanding some manifestation, burned Mezhenetskii's heart. He could not sit in one place, could not calm down, could not drive away his thoughts.

"How?" he began to put the question to himself. "Cut an artery? I can't. Hang myself? Of course, it's the simplest."

He remembered that there was a rope tied around a bundle of firewood that lay in the corridor. "Stand on the firewood or on a stool. The guard walks along the corridor. But he will go to sleep or go out. I'll have to wait, and then get the rope and attach it to the air vent."

Standing by his door, Mezhenetskii listened to the guard's steps in the corridor, and now and then, when the guard went away to the far end, he looked out through the aperture in the door. The guard still did not go away or go to sleep. Mezhenetskii listened avidly to the sounds of his steps and waited.

Meanwhile, in the cell where the sick old man was, amid the darkness that was scarcely lit by a smoking lamp, amid the drowsy, nocturnal sounds of breathing, grumbling, groaning, snoring, and coughing, the greatest thing in the world was occurring. The old schismatic was dying, and to his spiritual gaze was revealed everything that he had sought and desired so passionately throughout his entire life. Amid blinding light he saw the Lamb in the form of the radiant youth. A great number of people from all nations stood in front of him in white garments, and they all rejoiced, for there was no more evil on earth. All this happened, as the old man knew, both in his soul and in the whole world, and he felt great joy and calm.

The people in the cell only heard the old man loudly wheeze

his death rattle. His neighbor woke up and aroused the others, and when the wheezing ceased and the old man became silent and cold, they began to knock on the door.

The guard unlocked the door and entered. In ten minutes two prisoners carried out the dead body and took it down to the mortuary. The guard went out after them, locking the door behind him. The corridor was empty.

"Lock it, lock it," thought Mezhenetskii, who followed everything that happened from his door. "Do not prevent me from getting out of all this absurd horror."

Mezhenetskii no longer felt that inner horror that had tormented him before. Now he was engrossed in one concern: that something might prevent him from carrying out his intention.

With palpitating heart he went over to the bundle of firewood, untied the rope, pulled it out from under the wood, and, looking around at the door, took it to his cell. In his cell he stepped onto the stool and threw the rope around the air vent. Having tied together both ends of the rope, he pulled the knot, and with the doubled rope he made a noose. The noose was too low. He tied the rope anew, made a noose again, and tried it on his neck. Then, anxiously listening and looking at the door, he stepped onto the stool, put his head into the noose, adjusted it, and, pushing the stool away, hung. . . .

Only on his morning round did the guard see Mezhenetskii, standing on legs bent at the knees near a stool that was lying on its side. They took him out of the noose. The inspector came running, and having learned that Roman was a doctor, he called him to help the strangled man.

All the usual methods of resuscitation were applied, but Mezhenetskii did not come to life.

They took Mezhenetskii's body down to the mortuary and laid it on a plank bed next to the body of the old schismatic.

Berries

Hot, windless June days have come. The leaves in the wood are lush, thick, and green; only here and there some birch and lime leaves have turned yellow and are falling. Sweetbriar bushes are strewn with fragrant flowers; the meadows by the wood are covered with honey clover; thick, tall rye, which has half ripened, is turning dark and rippling. In the hollows corncrakes are calling to one another; in the oats and rye quails now wheeze and now trill; the nightingale in the wood will only now and then sing snatches of song and fall silent. The dry heat is baking. On the roads the dry dust lies motionless to a finger's depth and rises in a thick cloud, which is carried now to the right and now to the left by a slight, fortuitous puff.

The peasants complete their building and cart manure. The cattle on the dried-up fallow are hungry, waiting for the after-grass. Cows and calves low with their tails raised crookedly, as they run out of their stall and away from the herdsmen. Children watch the horses on the roads and edges. Women drag sacks of grass from the wood; lasses and little girls in rivalry with one another crawl among the bushes in the felled wood, gathering berries, which they take to the villas to sell to the residents.

The residents of the decorated and architecturally pretentious houses stroll lazily under parasols, in light, clean, expensive clothes, along paths strewn with sand, or sit in the shade of trees and arbors at small painted tables and, languishing with the heat, drink tea and soft drinks.

At Nikolai Semenych's splendid villa, with a tower, a verandah, a balcony, and galleries—where everything is fresh and new and clean—there stands a carriage with a troika of stage horses with bells, which has brought a Petersburg gentleman from the town for fifteen "smackers," as the coachman says.

This gentleman is a well-known liberal who has taken part in all the committees, commissions, and submissions, which are cunningly composed so as to appear loyal, and in essentially the most liberal petitions. He has come from the town, in which, as always, he is a terribly busy man, and will stay for only twenty-four hours with his friend, a childhood companion who holds almost the same views.

They differ only a little about the means of applying constitutional principles. The Petersburger is more European, with a slight inclination even toward socialism, and receives a very large salary for the positions he occupies. Nikolai Semenych is a pure Russian, Orthodox, with a Slavophile coloring, and owns many thousands of *desyatinas* of land.

They had a five-course dinner in the garden, but because of the heat they ate almost nothing, so that the labors of the forty-rouble cook and his assistants, who had worked particularly zealously for the guest, were almost wasted. They ate only chilled *botvinnia* with fresh white salmon and many-colored ice cream in a beautiful form and embellished with a variety of spun sugar and sponge cake. The diners were the guest, a liberal doctor, a tutor—a student, a desperate Social Democrat, a revolutionary, whom Nikolai Semenych was able to keep in check—Mary, Nikolai Semenych's wife, and three children, the youngest of whom had come only for the dessert.

The dinner was a little strained, because Mary, a very nervous woman, was worried about Goga's stomach disorder—so the youngest boy, Nikolai, was called (as was the custom among respectable people)—and also because, as soon as a political discussion began between the guest and Nikolai Semenych, the desperate student, wishing to show that he was not ashamed to express his convictions in front of anyone, burst into the conversation, and the guest fell silent. But Nikolai Semenych calmed the revolutionary down.

They dined at seven o'clock. After dinner the friends sat on the verandah, refreshing themselves with cold Narzan and a light white wine, and talked.

The difference among them first of all appeared in the question whether the elections should be in two stages or in one, and they were on the point of arguing hotly when they were called to tea in the dining room, which was protected against flies with nets. At tea they had a general conversation with Mary, who could not be interested in it as she was wholly absorbed in her thoughts about the signs of Goga's stomach disorder. The conversation was about painting, and Mary maintained that in decadent painting there was a *je ne sais quoi* that could not be denied. She was not thinking at all about decadent painting at that moment but was saying what she had said many times. The guest did not need any of this, but hearing that they were speaking against decadence, he spoke so similarly that no one would have suspected that he had nothing to do with decadence or nondecadence. Nikolai Semenych, looking at his wife, felt that she was dissatisfied with something and that there was, perhaps, going to be some unpleasantness—besides that, he was very bored with listening to what she was saying and what he had heard, it seemed to him, more than a hundred times.

Expensive bronze lamps and lanterns were lit in the courtyard, and the children were put to bed, the sick Goga having been subjected to medical treatment.

The guest, Nikolai Semenych, and the doctor went out onto the verandah. A footman brought candles with shades and some more Narzan, and about twelve o'clock there began a regular, animated discussion about what measures the government should take at the present time, which was so important for Russia. Both the guest and Nikolai Semenych smoked incessantly while they talked.

Outside, beyond the gate of the villa the coach horses were rattling their bells, standing without food, and the old coachman sitting in the carriage also without food now yawned and now snored. He had lived for twenty years with one master and sent all his wages home to his brother, except for three or five roubles, which he spent on drink. When the cocks began to crow from the various villas, and there was a particularly loud and shrill one next door, the coachman, wondering if they had forgotten him, got out of the carriage and went into the villa. He saw that his fare was sitting and drinking something and speaking loudly at intervals. He got worried and went to find the footman. The footman was asleep in the anteroom, sitting in his livery coat. The coachman woke him up. The footman, formerly a manor serf, supported his large family—five girls and two boys—by his service (which was profitable—fifteen roubles in wages, and tips amounting sometimes to a hundred roubles a year). He jumped up, and having straightened his clothes and shaken himself, he went to the gentlemen to say that the coachman was worried and was asking to go.

When the footman entered, the argument was in full swing. The doctor had joined the others and was taking part.

"I cannot admit," the guest was saying, "that the Russian people should follow any other path of development. Before all, liberty is necessary—political liberty—liberty, as this is known to everyone, the greatest liberty that is consistent with observance of the greatest rights of other people."

The guest felt that he was getting confused and saying something wrong, but in the heat of the argument he could not well recollect how he should speak.

"That's so," answered Nikolai Semenych, who was not listening to his guest and wanted only to express his own idea, which he particularly liked. "That's so, but this can be achieved by another path—not by a majority vote, but by general consent. Look at the decisions of a village commune."

"Ah, the commune!"

"You can't deny," said the doctor, "that the Slavic peoples have their own particular point of view. For example, the Polish right of *veto*. I don't maintain that this was better."

"Allow me, I will tell you the whole of my idea," Nikolai Semenych began. "The Russian people have particular characteristics. These characteristics—"

But Ivan approached in his livery and with sleepy eyes and interrupted him:

"The coachman is worried. . . ."

"Tell him"—the guest from Petersburg used the second-person plural to all footmen and was proud of it—"that I will come soon. And I will pay him extra."

"Yes, sir."

Ivan went out, and Nikolai Semenych could tell them the whole of his idea. But both the guest and the doctor had heard it twenty times (or at least so it seemed to them), and they began, especially the guest, to refute it with examples from history. The guest's knowledge of history was excellent.

The doctor was on the guest's side and admired his erudition and was glad of the chance to get acquainted with him.

The conversation so dragged on that it began to grow light beyond the wood on the other side of the road and the nightingale awoke, but the collocutors still smoked and talked, talked and smoked.

Perhaps the conversation would have lasted even longer, but a housemaid came out through the door.

This housemaid was an orphan, who had to go into service in order to support herself. At first she lived in a mercantile house, where a salesman seduced her and she gave birth. When her child died, she went to work for an official, whose schoolboy son did not let her have any peace. Then she went to work as an assistant housemaid for Nikolai Semenych and considered herself fortunate, because the gentlemen did not pursue her with their lust and her wages were paid regularly. She came to announce that the lady was asking for the doctor and Nikolai Semenych.

"Oh," thought Nikolai Semenych, "I suppose there's something wrong with Goga."

"What is it?" he asked.

"Nikolai Nikolaevich is not very well," said the housemaid. Nikolai Nikolaevich and the third-person plural—this was Goga, who was afflicted with diarrhea and had overeaten.

"Well, it's time," said the guest. "Look how light it is. How long we've stayed up!" he said with a smile, as if congratulating himself and his collocutors on having talked so much and for so long, and he said good-bye.

For a long time Ivan ran about on weary legs, looking for the guest's hat and umbrella, which the guest himself had pushed into the most inappropriate places. Ivan hoped for a tip, but the guest, who was always generous and would in no way have regretted giving him a rouble, quite forgot about it, he was so carried away by the conversation, and only remembered on the road that he had not given anything to the footman. "Well, there's nothing I can do about it."

The coachman climbed onto the box, picked up the reins, sat down sideways, and touched the horses. Their bells rang. The Petersburger traveled, rocking on soft springs, and thought about his friend's narrow-mindedness and prejudice.

Nikolai Semenych, who did not go to his wife at once, thought the same. "This Petersburg narrow-mindedness is terrible. They can't get out of it," he thought.

He delayed going to his wife because he did not expect any good from this meeting now. The whole thing was about berries. Yesterday some boys brought some berries. Without bargaining, Nikolai Semenych bought two platefuls of berries that were not quite ripe. The children came running, asking for some, and began to eat straight from the plates. Mary had not yet gone out. When she went out and learned that Goga had been given some berries, she got terribly angry, since he already had a stomach disorder. She began to scold her husband, and he her. An unpleasant talk, almost a quarrel, ensued. Toward evening Goga had the runs. Nikolai Semenych thought that this was the end of it, but calling the doctor meant that the thing had taken a bad turn.

When he went to his wife, she was wearing a brightly colored silk dressing gown, which she liked very much but which she was not thinking about now, and was standing in the nursery with the doctor over the pot and lighting it for him with a guttering candle.

The doctor, with an attentive expression and in pince-nez, was looking into it and stirring the stinking contents with a small stick.

"Yes," he said significantly.

"It's all those damned berries."

"Why the berries?" Nikolai Semenych said timidly.

"Why the berries? You fed him on them, that's why. But I can't sleep tonight, and the child will die. . . ."

"No, he won't die," said the doctor, smiling. "A little dose of bismuth and some care. We'll give him a dose now."

"He has fallen asleep," said Mary.

"Well, it's better not to disturb him. I'll call tomorrow."

"Please do."

The doctor went away. Nikolai Semenych stayed and was long unable to calm his wife. When he fell asleep, it was already quite light.

In the next village at the same time men and children were returning from a night watch. Some were on their own; others had horses in harness, with foals of one or two years running behind.

Taraska Rezunov, a little twelve-year-old, in a sheepskin coat and peaked cap, but barefoot, on a skewbald mare with a gelding in harness and a yearling as skewbald as its mother, outstripped everyone and galloped uphill toward the village. A black dog ran merrily in front of the horses, glancing back at them. The well-fed skewbald yearling kicked back with his legs in white stockings now to one side and now to the other. Taraska rode up to a hut, dismounted, tied the horses to the gate, and went into the passage.

"Hey, you, you've overslept!" he shouted to his sisters and brother, who were sleeping on a bit of sacking in the passage.

Their mother, who had been sleeping beside them, had already gotten up to milk the cow.

Olgushka jumped up, tidying her long, disheveled fair hair with both hands, but Fedka, who had been sleeping with her, still lay there with his head buried in a fur coat and only rubbed with a hardened heel a slender little leg that was sticking out from under a caftan.

The children had been gathering berries in the evening, and Taraska had promised to wake up his sisters and little brother as soon as he returned from the night watch.

So he did. While on the night watch, sitting under a bush, he had fallen asleep. Now he was wide awake and decided not to go to bed but to look for berries with the girls. His mother gave him a mug of milk. He cut off a chunk of bread for himself, sat at the table on a high bench, and began to eat.

Wearing just a shirt and trousers, and with quick steps making distinct prints of his bare feet in the dust, he went along the road, on which there were already several such footprints, some bigger and some smaller, with clearly printed toes. The girls could already be seen a long way in front as red-and-white specks against the dark green grove. (In the evening they had provided themselves with pots and mugs, and without breakfast and without taking any bread, they had crossed themselves twice in the front corner and run onto the street.) Taraska caught up with them beyond the forest just as they turned off the road.

Dew lay on the grass, on the bushes, and even on the lower branches of both bushes and trees. The girls' little bare feet immediately got wet and at first grew cold but then warmed up as they stepped now on the soft grass and now on the rough, dry soil. The place for berries was in the felled wood. The girls went first into last year's clearing. Young shoots were just rising, and between the succulent young bushes there stretched places with short grass, in which pinky white and here and there red berries were concealed as they ripened.

Bending double, the girls picked berry after berry with their little sunburned hands and put the worse ones into their mouths and the better ones into the mugs.

"Olgushka! Come here. Here are lots."

"What? No kidding? Halloo!" they shouted to each other, not moving far apart as they went behind the bushes.

Taraska went farther away from them beyond a ravine into a wood that had been felled a year earlier, and in which the young shoots, particularly of nut trees and maples, were higher than a man. The grass was lusher and thicker, and when he found places with strawberries, the berries were bigger and juicier under the protection of the grass.

"Grushka!"

"Hi!"

"What if a wolf comes?"

"What wolf? You're scaring me. But I reckon I'm not afraid," said Grushka, and thinking about the wolf, she absentmindedly picked berry after berry, putting the best ones not into a mug, but into her mouth.

"Our Taraska's gone beyond the ravine. Taraska-a!"

"Ya-oh!" Taraska answered from beyond the ravine. "Come here."

"We'll come. There're more there."

The girls climbed down into the ravine, holding on to the bushes, and from the ravine they climbed up by branches onto the other side, and there, right in the sun, they came at once upon a clearing with fine grass, strewn all over with berries. They were both silent and worked incessantly with both hands and lips.

Suddenly something dashed past and with a terrible din, as it seemed to them, amid the silence crashed through the grass and bushes.

Grushka fell down with fright and spilled half a mugful of berries that she had gathered.

"Mummy!" she squealed, and began to cry.

"It's a hare, a hare! Taraska! A hare. There it is!" cried Olgush-ka, pointing to a gray-brown back with ears, flashing among the bushes. "What's the matter?" Olgushka asked Grushka when the hare had disappeared.

"I thought it was a wolf," Grushka answered, and suddenly, straight after the horror and tears of despair, she burst out laughing.

"There's a silly."

"I was terribly frightened," said Grushka with a merry, ringing laugh like a bell.

They picked berries and went farther. The sun had risen and with bright, radiant spots and shadows colored the verdure and shone in the drops of dew, in which the girls were now soaked right up to their waists.

The girls were almost at the end of the wood, still going farther and farther away in the hope that the farther they went, the more berries there would be, when in various places were heard the ringing halloos of girls and women, who had come out later and were also gathering berries.

By breakfast time the mugs and pots were already half-full, when the girls met Aunt Akulina, who had also come out for berries. Behind Aunt Akulina a tiny, potbellied boy in just a shirt and without a cap toddled on fat, bandy little legs.

"I dragged him out with me," Akulina said to the girls as she took the boy in her arms. "There was no one to leave him with."

"We just frightened a big hare. How it crashed—scared . . ."

"Really?" said Akulina, and put the boy down again.

After chatting like this, the girls parted from Akulina and continued their task.

"Let's sit down now," said Olgushka, sitting in the thick shade of a nut bush. "I'm tired out. Eh, we didn't bring any bread. I'm hungry."

"So am I," said Grushka.

"What's that Aunt Akulina is shouting so loud? Can you hear? Halloo, Aunt Akulina!"

"Olgushka-a!" Akulina answered.

"What?"

"The boy isn't with you, is he?" Akulina shouted from beyond the branches.

"No."

The bushes began to rustle, and Aunt Akulina herself appeared from behind the branches, with her skirt tucked up above her knees and with a bag in her hand.

"You didn't see the boy?"

"No."

"What a sin! Mishka-a-a!"

"Mishka-a-a!"

No one answered.

"Oh, dear! he'll get lost. He'll wander into the forest."

Olgushka jumped up and went with Grushka to search on one side, and Aunt Akulina went to search on the other. They called Mishka incessantly with ringing voices, but no one responded.

"I'm tired out," said Grushka, lagging behind, but Olgushka hallooed incessantly and went now to the right and now to the left, looking on both sides.

Akulina's desperate voice was heard far away toward the forest. Olgushka was wanting to give up the search and go home, when in a lush bush, by the base of some young lime shoots, she heard the persistent, angry, and desperate chirp of some bird, probably with fledglings, that was dissatisfied with something. The bird was obviously afraid of and angry at something. Olgushka turned to look at the bush, which was overgrown with tall, thick grass with white flowers, and right under it she saw a blue heap, which did not resemble any grasses in the wood. She stopped and examined it. This was Mishka. It was him that the bird was afraid of and angry at.

Mishka lay on his fat belly, with his arms placed under his head and his plump, bandy legs stretched out, and slept sweetly.

Olgushka called his mother, and when she had woken up the little boy she gave him some berries.

For a long time afterward Olgushka told everyone she met and at home she told her mother and father and the neighbors how she had looked for and how she had found Akulina's little boy.

The sun had risen fully from behind the wood and with its heat scorched the earth and everything that was on it.

"Olgushka! Come for a swim," some girls who met Olga said invitingly, and they all went singing and dancing to the river.

Floundering, squealing, and dangling their legs, the girls did not notice how a low, black cloud was approaching from the west, how the sun was beginning to go in and come out, and how there came a scent of flowers and birch leaves and it began to thunder. The girls did not have time to get dressed before the rain came pouring down and soaked them to the skin.

The girls came running home in darkened smocks that clung to their bodies, had something to eat, and carried their father's dinner into the field, where he was plowing the potatoes.

When they had returned and had their dinner, their smocks were dry. Having sorted out the strawberries and put them into cups, they took them to Nikolai Semenych's villa, where the people paid well; but this time they refused.

Mary, sitting in a big armchair under an umbrella and languishing with the heat, when she saw the girls with berries waved her fan at them.

"No need, no need."

But Valya, the oldest boy, aged twelve, who was relaxing from the stress of his classical high school and playing croquet with the neighbors, when he saw the berries ran up to Olgushka and asked:

"How much?"

She said:

"Thirty copecks."

"That's a lot," he said. He said "That's a lot" because grown-ups always said that. "Wait; just go around the corner," he said, and ran to the nanny.

Meanwhile Olgushka and Grushka admired a glass ball, in which some little houses, woods, and gardens could be seen. This ball and much else were not surprising to them, because they expected all the most wonderful things in the mysterious and to them incomprehensible world of the gentlefolk.

Valya ran to the nanny and began asking her for thirty copecks. The nanny said that twenty were enough and got him the money from a box. Avoiding his father, who had only just gotten up after last night's exertion and was smoking and reading the newspapers, Valya gave a twenty-copeck coin to the girls, and having tipped the berries onto a plate, he fell to.

When Olgushka had returned home, she undid with her teeth a knot in her kerchief, in which the twenty-copeck coin had been tied, and gave it to her mother. Her mother hid the money and took the washing to the river.

Taraska, who had been plowing the potatoes with his father since breakfast, was sleeping at this time in the shade of a thick, dark oak. His father was sitting with him, looking now and then at the horse, which had been hobbled and unharnessed and which was grazing at the boundary of another man's land and could at any moment stray into the oats or into his meadows.

Everything in Nikolai Semenych's family was today as usual. Everything was in order. A breakfast of three courses was ready; the flies had long been eating it, but no one came because no one wanted to eat.

Nikolai Semenych was satisfied with the justice of his opinions, which was shown by what he read today in the newspapers. Mary was calm because Goga had had a good motion. The doctor was satisfied because the remedies that he had prescribed had worked. Valya was satisfied because he had eaten a whole plateful of strawberries.

»»» APPENDIX «««
SIBIR I KATORGA (SIBERIA AND PENAL SERVITUDE) BY SERGEI MAXIMOV

The following translated excerpts are from Sergei Maximov's Sibir i
Katorga, *a three-volume sociological treatise published in St. Petersburg in 1871.*

The *ksiądz* Sirocynski, formerly a prior at the Church of St. Basil
in Ovruch (in Volhynia), was deprived of his ecclesiastical rank
for taking part in the November insurrection and, having become
a simple Cossack instead of a prior, found himself at Omsk. When
a Cossack college was founded here and a teacher was needed, it
was remembered that Sirocynski had been a professor and inspector of schools. He was given the position and with it the greatest
freedom. In freedom he became friends with an exiled doctor Szokalski and established a large secret society among the Poles who
had been banished to line and Cossack regiments. The aim of the
conspiracy was to try to tear Siberia away from Russia, to free all
the "unfortunates" from heavy penal servitude, and to stir up the
settlers in the places of their establishment. Omsk, with its artillery supplies, ammunition, weapons, financial exchequer, and so
on, aroused a strong temptation. Both Tatars and Russians, free
men and slaves, managed to join this society. It was arranged that
in the event of the failure of the great uprising, they would all
flee, with arms in their hands, across the Kirgiz steppe to Tash-
kent, where many Catholics were supposed to be, and to Bukhara.
From here, if final necessity required it, they would make their

way to British India. Up to two thousand Poles gathered in Omsk and its environs. The Kirgiz steppe, just on the far side of the Irtysh, lured with an irresistible temptation the seekers of strong sensations and adventures.

The revolution was to begin on the next day in the evening. But there were three Poles, soldiers in the insurrection of 1830 (Knak from Warsaw and the Gaewskis from Congress Poland), who appeared before Colonel Degrav and told him everything: that the conspiracy had spread to the most distant parts of Siberia, that it met with sympathy in the most remote places, and that if prompt and decisive measures were not taken, it would envelop the whole country and certainly succeed. They named Sirocynski as the leader and many accomplices as having the greatest power, influence, and significance. All these, whether they lived in Omsk or in its nearest environs, were immediately arrested. The strictest orders were issued, and instructions were sent to the most distant parts of western Siberia for the arrest by the quickest means of all suspects and influential persons: Russians, Poles, Siberians, soldiers, settlers, peasants. Up to a thousand people were first seized. Dr. Szokalski, the Pole Zubczewski, and the Russian Melodin managed to slip away on the first day of the arrests and flee along the post road to the province of Orenburg. On the road Szokalski played the role of an army doctor, Zubczewski of his assistant, and Melodin of his servant. The fugitives were recognized at the Presnovskaya *stanitsa*, and they were returned under a strong escort to Omsk, where an investigation was in full swing at that time. The arrests were carried out at the end of 1834 and the beginning of 1835. The affair was made known in Petersburg. Two commissions of inquiry, one after the other, puzzled over the affair and were dissolved without having reached any decision. A third commission was sent from Petersburg; it worked for three years and brought the investigation to a conclusion. Some, because of their innocence, were set at liberty; those acknowledged to be guilty were brought to trial. Pending the trial, the chief culprit did not lose heart. In prison he wrote poetry; in court he did not reveal anything, just as at the inquiry nothing could be learned from him. "One day my mother bore—one day to be no more," said Sirocynski, repeating his Ukrainian saying to everyone. His poems were distributed among the Siberian Poles; he enlivened them with his energy; he raised the hopes and strengthened the patriotic spirit of the slaves.

The affair had begun on a large scale and filled the whole of Siberia with fear. Under the influence of this fear, even on the termination of the affair the Poles were suspected and persecuted. At the Presnovskaya *stanitsa* the Poles were suspected of arson and of designs to continue with Sirocynski's plans. Four were punished with exile to the Ust-Kamenogorsk fortress, where they were compelled to work in irons for five years, and in 1845 they were sent as soldiers to Nerchinsk. On the termination of the Omsk affair, Poles began to be transferred from factories in western Siberia to factories in eastern Siberia. In Irkutsk there was such a fear of arson that the Polish soldiers in the garrison there were surrounded with the strictest supervision. Their comrades in arms were ordered to have their guns loaded and to confine all the Poles to barracks as soon as the ringing of the alarm bell was heard. Many of the Poles on suspicion were locked in the guard-houses; many were sent away to Transbaikal towns: to Ver-khneudinsk and Kyakhta. Pyrophobia in Siberia had never been so general and so dangerous as at this time. Every fire was attributed to arson by the Poles. Fear managed even to pass from Siberia beyond the Ural range and spread across Russia. The position of the political offenders deteriorated. In 1846 a particularly strong movement among all the exiles gave rise to the prohibition to hold property. If an informality occurred at the release of some convicts, they were ordered to return again to penal servitude. So all those who had served ten years but had been banished for twenty, and who had gotten married and acquired household effects, were obliged to return to penal servitude again to work for ten years.

Sentences for the Omsk affair were passed as follows. Six were condemned to seven thousand blows of the cane and then ordered to be sent for the rest of their lives to hard labor in the Nerchinsk mines. The others were condemned to three, two, or one thousand blows of the cane, or of birch rods, and then the foremost to hard labor for the rest of their lives, or for a limited number of years, or straight to a settlement. The remainder were ordered to be sent to various distant Siberian battalions and detachments. The day appointed for the flogging, March 7, 1837, was frosty. On the square behind the town, which was covered with snow, two battalions of a thousand soldiers were drawn up, armed with canes of such thickness that only three could go into the muzzle of a gun. The battalions were lined up, stretched out, contrary to regulations, in widely placed ranks. The soldiers ought to have stood at ease in close order, and when striking they ought not to have moved their elbows far from their sides or advanced their feet from the lines. First Szokalski was led with his back stripped to the waist and with his hands tied to the butt of a gun and held by two noncommissioned officers. A doctor who was present at the flogging pleaded for his fellow and, going behind him, whispered to the soldiers to beat more lightly, to have compassion: he was feeble and sick and would not endure it. When Szokalski fell after five thousand blows, and when he did not consent to his colleague's advice to go through with the last thousand and so complete the flogging, the doctor insisted that they stop the punishment and send the sick man to the infirmary. Sirocynski was led last. He did not take any styptic drops as he approached the ranks. When he heard the order to commence, he began to recite in a singsong the penitential psalm *Miserere mei Deus secundum magnam misericordiam tuam* and so on. Weak, emaciated in incarceration, Sirocynski did not endure the punishment; other comrades did not endure it, either. Having rested in the infirmary, Szokalski then went through with the last thousand and the next day was taken away to the Nerchinsk mines [3:63–67].

[Maximov tells how Dr. Szokalski, who lived by trade in the Kara district, treated convicts and rich people, day and night, free of charge. He devised a plan of mass escape, but when this proved impossible he became melancholic and committed suicide by shooting himself. He was mourned by his dog (67–68).]

Not only do natural boundaries and various places transmit legends about the unsuccessful attempts of the Poles, but even tombstones in Polish cemeteries in Siberia eloquently and persistently speak of how the history of Polish exiles is speckled with escapes, and how not a little effort and time were spent on them in vain, not only in Siberia, but also in Russia. In (Great) Nerchinskii Zavod one such tombstone covers the grave of Albina Migurska—a true heroine in the whole history of Polish slavery. This young woman despised all social connections and the wealth of her parents, and did not pay attention to the advice of her relatives and friends or to the hardships of a long journey and the sorrows of her future, but went to her fiancé in the town of Uralsk, where he had been exiled as a soldier in a line battalion. Here she married him and became a true delight for him and a guiding star in the gloomy night of slavery. She bore two children, but the children soon died, leaving to their mother the old melancholy in her heart and a strengthened desire to free her husband and herself from slavery. One day some Cossacks brought to her from the bank of the Ural her husband's clothes and a letter, in which he asked for her forgiveness for the misfortune to which he had subjected her, having thrown himself into the water from homesickness and having left her in an uncertain position in a strange land. The grief and tears of the unfortunate woman were so sincere and compelling that all the Uralsk ladies and authorities had the most heartfelt concern for Migurska. Their visits were frequent and of long duration, and at last began to torment her, because her husband, hidden in the next room, could at any moment betray her with a sneeze, a cough, or some untimely movement. She endured infernal torture all the time while her request for permission to return to her native land was being processed. The secret was preserved; even the maidservant who had been brought from Poland was able to keep it sacred. When permission for departure was received, Migurska expressed a desire to exhume her children's corpses from Cossack soil and take their bones away to Polish soil. She laid these bones in one coffin, and there she hid her husband. For the journey a Cossack was assigned to her as an escort. The coffin with the live Migurski was placed under the driver's seat, and in this way he traveled safely out of the bounds of the Uralsk army. In the province of Saratov the Cossack managed to overhear a conversation between the husband and wife and reported this to the authorities. The husband and wife arrived at Saratov as prisoners, and there still to this day that startling moment is remembered when the Migurskis went into the *kościół* and fell on their knees in front of their children's coffin: she in mourning, he in irons. Migurska became a subject of conversation; the Poles there regarded her as a saint, soliciting her on their knees for a blessing. A manifesto on the occasion of the wedding of the reigning sovereign emperor freed Migurski from punishment. He was sent not to labor, but only to the Siberian army, and was stationed at Nerchinskii Zavod. Here Migurska fell into a consumption and died [3:75–76].

Preface

1. Leo Tolstoy, *What Is Art?* (1898), in *What Is Art? and Essays on Art,* translated by Aylmer Maude (London: Oxford University Press, 1955), 123.

2. Ibid., 196–97.

Translator's Introduction

1. *Tolstoy's Diaries,* edited and translated by R. F. Christian, 2 vols. (London: Athlone Press, 1985), January 2, March 29, May 30, 1904; October 23, November 3 and 22, December 9, 1905.

2. Ibid., December 13, 1897; December 30, 1903.

3. Ibid., June 12, 1905.

4. Ibid., January 22, February 2, 6, and 18, March 2, April 25, 1906.

5. L. N. Tolstoi, *Sobranie Sochinenii v Dvenadtsati Tomakh,* edited by S. A. Makashin and L. D. Opulskaya, vol. 11 (Moscow: Pravda, 1987), 570–71.

6. Ibid., 571–72; Franco Venturi, *Roots of Revolution: A History of the Populist and Socialist Movements in Nineteenth-Century Russia,* translated from the Italian by Francis Haskell, introduction by Isaiah Berlin (London: Weidenfeld and Nicolson, 1960), 635–37.

7. *Sobranie Sochinenii,* 11:572.

8. Leo Tolstoy, "Introduction to an Examination of the Gospels," in *A Confession, The Gospel in Brief and What I Believe,* translated and with an introduction by Aylmer Maude (London: Oxford University Press, 1958), 108.

9. Hans Rogger, *Russia in the Age of Modernisation and Revolution, 1881–1917* (London and New York: Longman, 1983), 134, 142, 151–52; W. Bruce Lincoln, *In War's Dark Shadow: The Russians before the Great War* (New York: Dial Press, 1983), 160–85; Alan Wood, *The Origins of the Russian Revolution, 1861–1917,* 2d ed. (London and New York: Routledge, 1993), 20–21, 26–27.

10. Leo Tolstoy, "Thou Shalt Not Kill," in *Recollections and Essays,* translated and with an introduction by Aylmer Maude (London: Oxford University Press, 1952), 196, 201, 203.

11. Leo Tolstoy, "A Great Iniquity," in *Recollections and Essays,* 272–73, 305.

12. Leo Tolstoy, *On Life,* in *On Life and Essays on Religion,* translated and with an introduction by Aylmer Maude (London: Oxford University Press, 1950), 148–60.

13. G. V. Plekhanov, "A Confusion of Ideas," in *L. N. Tolstoi v Russkoi Kritike: Sbornik Statei,* 3d ed., edited by S. P. Bychkov (Moscow: Gosudarstvennoe Izdatelstvo Khudozhestvennoi Literatury, 1960), 344.

14. *What I Believe,* 457.

15. Leo Tolstoy, *What Then Must We Do?* translated by Aylmer Maude (London: Oxford University Press, 1950), 110; Leo Tolstoy, *The Kingdom of God Is within You,* in *The Kingdom of God and Peace Essays,* translated and with an introduction by Aylmer Maude (London: Oxford University Press, 1951), 208; "A Great Iniquity," 273.

16. Sophocles, *Oedipus Tyrannus,* 1186–96.

17. *On Life*, title of chapter 1.

18. "Christianity and Patriotism," in *The Kingdom of God and Peace Essays*, 509–10.

19. R. F. Leslie, *Polish Politics and the Revolution of November 1830* (London: Athlone Press, University of London, 1956), 51, 54, 69–72, quoting P. Harro-Harring, *Poland under the Dominion of Russia* (London, 1831), 255–56.

20. Leslie, *Polish Politics and the Revolution of November 1830*, 177–78, 227–29.

21. G. W. Spence, *Tolstoy the Ascetic* (Edinburgh and London: Oliver and Boyd, 1967), 103–5.

22. S. Maximov, *Sibir i Katorga*, 3 vols. (St Petersburg, 1871), 1:345.

What For?

3   *the spring of 1830*   Poland adopted the Gregorian calendar in 1586, but in Russia it was not adopted until 1918.

3   *Pan Jaczewski*   *Pan* is the Polish for "Mr." or "sir," *pani* for "Mrs." or "madam." *Paniusia* and *panienka*, which occur later in this story, mean "young lady" or "miss."

3   *Rzeczpospolita*   The republic or commonwealth, a federation of communities united by a single diet and an elected king. In the eighteenth century the republic consisted of the kingdom of Poland and the grand duchy of Lithuania.

    Stanisław August Poniatowski, former lover of Catherine the Great, who chose him as king of Poland, was elected and crowned in 1764. Patriots considered him to be a traitor because, after swearing to the constitution of May 3, 1791, which alarmed the Russian empress, he abandoned it in the following year, when the Russian army invaded Poland.

In calling Catherine II "the apocalyptic whore," Jaczewski refers to Revelation 17:1–6.

Poland was partitioned in 1772, 1793, and 1795. Land was seized by Russia, Prussia, and Austria, though Austria had no share in the second partition, in which the other two powers took half the population and half the territory of the republic.

Lieutenant General Tadeusz Kościuszko led a national insurrection against the Russian and Prussian forces in Poland in 1794. He won a famous victory on April 4 in his first battle, at Racławice near Cracow, where he led peasants armed with scythes against a Russian battery. This was followed by successes in Warsaw and Lithuania. But after subsequent losses the Poles were decisively defeated on October 10 at Maciejowice, where Kościuszko was taken prisoner. On November 4 the Russians stormed Praga near Warsaw and massacred the inhabitants. This was followed by the third partition, by which the remnant of Poland was seized by the three powers, who agreed to abolish everything that might even recall the existence of a Polish kingdom.

3   *the army of Napoleon* After Napoleon had defeated the Prussians at Jena in 1806, the Poles rose against the Prussian garrisons, and he entered Warsaw in triumph in January 1807. Polish troops played a distinguished part in the French victory over the Russian army at Friedland in June. The Russian emperor, Alexander I, formed an alliance with Napoleon in July 1807. By the Treaty of Tilsit the Prussian king had to recognize the duchy of Warsaw, which Napoleon had created and which was given a Napoleonic constitution with the king of Saxony at its head. A Polish army, formed on the French model, defended the duchy against an Austrian attack in 1809. A decisive event was Napoleon's

defeat of the Austrians at Wagram in the same year, so that by the Treaty of Schönbrunn the whole of ex-Austrian western Galicia, including Cracow, was added to the ex-Prussian land that formed the duchy.

More than eighty thousand Polish soldiers took part in Napoleon's Russian campaign in 1812. He entered Moscow, but finding the city deserted and in flames, he withdrew and lost his army in his retreat during winter.

3   *The opening of the Sejm . . . tyranny*   By the Treaty of Vienna, signed in 1815, the duchy of Warsaw became the Polish kingdom (often called the Congress Kingdom) with the Russian emperor as king—except for some territories returned to Prussia, and Cracow and its district, which were to be independent. Alexander promulgated a constitution establishing a Sejm (diet or parliament) of two houses, which was to meet for one month every two years, ministers appointed by the Crown, and a national defense force, of which Grand Duke Konstantin was commander in chief. Alexander opened the first session of the Sejm on March 27, 1818.

Under Konstantin the army was organized on the Russian model, which meant that corporal punishment, abolished at the time of the duchy, was reintroduced. The army was pervaded by spies of the secret police. Konstantin was so insulting to some officers that they committed suicide.

The Holy Alliance, which had been signed by the Russian and Austrian emperors and the Prussian king, was proclaimed by Alexander on September 26, 1815. All Christian sovereigns were invited to join the alliance, which would commit them to government according to Christian principles. The agreement was signed by all the sovereigns of Europe except the prince regent, the pope, and the Turkish sultan.

4   *szlachta*   The nobility and gentry.

4   *Wilno*   Vilnius.

4   *lui tenir la dragée haute*   "To tantalize him so that he would value her." Literally this French expression means "to hold the sweetmeat high for him."

5   *ksiądz*   A Roman Catholic priest.

6   *the Parisian revolution*   In July 1830, after King Charles X had dissolved the newly elected Chamber of Deputies, he was overthrown and replaced by Louis Philippe, who became the "citizen king" on August 7.

6   *the Polish people were again free*   The uprising that was begun in Warsaw on November 29, 1830, by a secret association of officers and pupils at the school of infantry cadets, encouraged by romantic intellectuals, was soon joined by the urban lower classes and by other soldiers. The insurgents failed to capture Grand Duke Konstantin when they attacked Belvedere Palace. Saying that he did not want to intervene, he refused to use his troops, who all belonged to the Lithuanian army corps, to put down the rebellion, and he was allowed to leave the kingdom with them. General Chłopicki, who was appointed commander in chief, tried to restore order in the hope that the conflict could be resolved peacefully and proclaimed himself dictator on December 5. But the Sejm, confirming his dictatorial powers on December 20, resolved to declare that the insurrection was national. Chłopicki resigned on January 17, being opposed to war and finding himself to be a dictator only on paper. The Sejm deposed the king, Nicholas I, by acclamation on January 25. This gave him the right under the Treaty of Vienna to send an army into the kingdom to enforce submission.

Alexander, Konstantin, and Nicholas were sons of Emperor Paul; hence the patronymic Pavlovich. Romanov was the family name.

6   *Jewish agents . . . affairs*   Many Jews supported the insurrection because Nicholas had included the Jews in the compulsory military service, which lasted ten years, and sought to convert them to Eastern Orthodoxy.

6   *the revolutionary committee*   On January 30, 1831, the Sejm granted supreme authority to a national government of five people, presided over by Prince Adam Czartoryski. This government resigned on August 16.

7   *the Poles' victory at Stoczek*   At Stoczek on February 14 General Dwernicki defeated the troops of General Geismar, who had approached from the southeast, but the Russians continued to advance from the northeast.

7   *Zwycięstwo . . . ! Wiwat!*   "Victory for the Poles and defeat for the Muscovites! Hurrah!"

7   *konfederatka*   Polish national or military headgear, a rectangular cap without a peak.

8   *now of Diebitsch . . . Paskevich*   Russian forces commanded by Field Marshal Diebitsch had advanced into Poland early in February 1831. After his death of cholera on June 10, his place was taken by Field Marshal Count Paskevich.

8   *Warsaw was taken*   Warsaw was abandoned to Paskevich on the night of September 7, 1831.

9   *returned to Russia*   It appears that Rożanka was in one of the former eastern provinces of Poland, which had become part of the western Russian empire.

14   *galloped through Russia . . . horses*   This refers to Nicholas's tours of inspection, which included the random enforcement of discipline. Chuguev is now Chuhuyiv, a town near Kharkiv on the river Siverskyy Donets.

15   *Decembrists*   The Decembrists were noblemen and gentlemen who were mostly military officers and who were patriotic, liberal intellectuals. They were all opposed to autocracy and serf-

dom, but in other respects there was a wide range of opinions among them. They had a northern society based on St. Petersburg and a southern society based on Tulchin. The latter made contact with the Polish Patriotic Society in January 1824. The Decembrists took their name from the uprising that occurred on December 14, 1825, when Nicholas had himself proclaimed emperor. More than two thousand mutineers occupied Senate Square in St. Petersburg, calling for Konstantin and a constitution. This revolt was put down by troops under Nicholas's command. A revolt in the south was overcome on January 3, 1826. Five of the Decembrists were hanged, and thirty-one were exiled for life with hard labor in Siberia.

15 *metallic eyes* Tolstoy rejected the custom of referring to czars' eyes as "radiant eyes." He did the same with the "glassy gaze" of Alexander II in "Divine and Human," section 1.

18 *Miserere mei . . . tuam* "Pity me, God, according to thy great mercy." This is a Latin version of Psalm 51, which is sung in the mass.

20 *tarantass* A springless carriage.

22 *Jak mamę kocham* "As true as I'm alive." Literally this Polish expression means "as I love Mama."

22 *a troika of horses* Three horses harnessed abreast.

23 *susliks* A genus of rodents of the family *Sciuridae*.

26 *Tsaritsyn* Volgograd.

27 *Obshchii Syrt* An upland forming the divide between the basins of the Volga and Ural Rivers.

28 *Pugachev* Emelyan Pugachev, a Don Cossack, led a rebellion that began in 1773 among the Yaik Cossacks (who lived by the river Yaik, since renamed the Ural). He claimed to be the deposed emperor Peter III, who would free the people from the oppression that they suffered under the usurper, Catherine II. He soon gained a large following among serfs,

factory workers, subject peoples, and religious schismatics, as the insurrection spread over a wide area of the Urals and the Volga. The insurrection was put down with cruel reprisals in the following year, and Pugachev was executed in Moscow in January 1775.

28   *Old Believer*   The Old Believers broke with the Russian Church when it was reformed by Nikon, who was patriarch from 1652 to 1667.

28   *sotenniks*   A *sotennik* is a measure of length or area equal to 100 *sazhens,* or square *sazhens.* A *sazhen* is 2.13 meters.

30   *Jak Boga kocham*   "As true as I'm alive." Literally this Polish expression means "as I love God."

Divine and Human

33   *The governor-general of the southern region*   By a decree of April 5, 1879, a governor-general with special powers was appointed in Odessa (now Odesa). Like other governor-generals, Count Eduard Totleben had distinguished himself in the recent Russo-Turkish war. By the middle of August he was responsible for the hanging of eight people, including Dmitrii Lizogub. One of the capital offenses was being in possession of dynamite, of which Lizogub was not guilty.

34   *Ein jeder . . . schlafen*   "As you make your bed so you must sleep on it" (German).

35   *Je deviens . . . engeance*   "I get wild when I think of that damned brood" (French).

38   *gendarmes*   The Corps of Gendarmes was the political police. It was attached to the Third Section of the Imperial Chancellery until August 1880, when it was transferred to the Department of State Police.

39   *the Kiev fortress*   There was a gun battle between police and revolutionaries in Kiev on the night of February 11, 1879.

41   *radiant life*   A play on Svetlogub's name. The word *svetlyi* means "light," "bright," or "radiant."

42   *The book of the generation . . . Abiud*   Matthew 1:1–2, 13.

42   *Gogol's Petrushka*   Petrushka, Chichikov's valet in *Dead Souls,* read books avidly regardless of their content because he enjoyed the process of reading.

43   *Blessed are they . . . men*   Matthew 5:10–13.

43   *Then said Jesus . . . soul?*   Matthew 16:24–26.

47   *Forgive them . . . do*   Luke 23:34.

50   *Verily, verily . . . fruit*   John 12:24.

51   *the Nikonian Church*   Nikon was patriarch of the Russian Church from 1652 to 1667. He reformed the Church, but many of the clergy opposed his innovations, and a schism occurred. The Old Believers, who broke with the official church, differed among themselves and split into groups with priests and groups without priests.

51   *Peter*   Peter the Great, autocratic ruler of Russia from 1696 to 1725, carried out extensive reforms in social and political life, expanding the rights of landowners over their serfs, promoting the rise of industry and commerce, creating a bureaucracy, dividing the country into provinces with governors, strengthening the armed forces, and bringing the church under state control.

51   *He that is unjust . . . be*   Revelation 22:11–12.

55   *Move here a bit farther*   In saying this, the hangman first uses the familiar form, like the French *tu,* but then corrects himself, using the respectful form, like the French *vous.*

56   *Into thy hands . . . spirit*   Luke 23:46.

58   *the blowing up of the czar's train*   The organization called the People's Will, formed in 1879, attempted this three times in November that year, when the czar traveled from the Crimean coast to Moscow.

59 *he corrected himself* Mezhenetskii has used a foreign word, "exploit."

60 *the public procurator* Public prosecutor.

63 *flogging* The punishment of running the gauntlet (known by its German name, *Spitzruten*), described in "What For?" was abolished by Alexander II in April 1863, but this was not the end of corporal punishment. The revolutionary Alexei Emelyanov, known as Bogolyubov, was flogged in July 1877 in the Remand Prison in St. Petersburg for refusing to take his cap off to General Fedor Trepov. This caused a mutiny in the prison and widespread indignation outside it.

64 *Nevskii to Nadezhdinskaya* Nevskii Prospekt is the main street in St. Petersburg. Nadezhdinskaya has been renamed Ulitsa Mayakovskogo; it extends northward from Nevskii Prospekt between Liteinyi Prospekt and Zamenskaya Ploshchad.

66 *Kropotkin, Mezentsov, and even Alexander II* General Mezentsov, chief of the gendarmes, was stabbed to death on August 4, 1878, by Sergei Kravchinskii, a member of the group called Land and Freedom. Dmitrii Kropotkin, governor of Kharkov (now Kharkiv), was shot dead on February 9, 1879, by Gregory Goldenberg, a Jewish member of the People's Will. The emperor Alexander II was killed by the People's Will on March 1, 1881, when a bomb was thrown by the Russified Pole Ignacy Hryniewiecki.

66 *reaction . . . Alexander III* A "regulation on measures for the protection of the system of government and of the public peace, and on the placement of certain of the empire's localities under a state of reinforced safeguard," which was introduced in August 1881 and renewed every three years, gave arbitrary powers to governors and the political police. The Department of Police and the Corps of Gendarmes, which were not answerable to the judiciary, could detain and exile individuals on suspicion and, by a decree of March 1882, subject them to overt surveillance. It was a crime to interfere in politics.

67   *Kautsky*   Karl Kautsky, born in Prague in 1854, became the editor in 1883 of *Die Neue Zeit,* the theoretical journal of the German Social Democratic movement. During the 1880s he wrote books and articles that propagated Marxist ideas, such as *The Economic Doctrine of Karl Marx* (1887).

68   *The first of March*   Alexander II was assassinated on March 1, 1881.

70   *The Lamb shall overcome . . . faithful*   Revelation 17:14.

70   *And there are seven czars . . . space*   Revelation 17:10. "Czars" instead of "kings" is the only departure from the Authorized King James Version in the translation of these quotations from the New Testament.

70   *Surely I come quickly. . . . Jesus*   Revelation 22:20.

71   *Khalturin, Kibalchich, and Perovskaya*   Stepan Khalturin, a member of the People's Will, caused an explosion in the Winter Palace on February 5, 1880, in a vain attempt to kill the czar. Nikolai Kibalchich, who was an explosives expert of the People's Will, and Sofya Perovskaya were conspirators in the successful plot of the following year and were hanged on April 3, 1881.

71   *he had taken away their serfs*   Alexander II emancipated the serfs in 1861.

Berries

76   *Slavophile* Slavophilism was developed in the late 1830s and 1840s in reaction against Westernization. The Slavophiles advocated a return to ancient Russian culture, with the village commune as the basis of society and with the faith of an ideal Orthodox Church. They valued community, psychic wholeness, and freedom from the state. In the following decades, particularly with the Crimean War and the Russo-Turkish War of 1877 to 1878, Slavophilism changed into Pan-Slavism, according to which it was hoped that the Slav peoples would be united under the benevolent Russian eagle.

76   *desyatinas* One *desyatina* equals 2.7 acres, or 1.0927 hectares.

76   *botvinnia* Cold fish-and-vegetable soup.

77   *Narzan* A mineral water.

77   *whether the elections . . . one* In the summer of 1905 there were widespread demands for a constituent assembly or at least for a legislature to be elected by universal, direct, equal, and secret vote. But on August 6 the government announced that the state Duma, which was to be only a consultative assembly, was to be elected by indirect and unequal vote. This meant that deputies were to be chosen by electors, who had themselves been chosen by certain sections of the population.

77   *je ne sais quoi* "I don't know what" (French), the elusive touch of genius. Some of the decadent painters were de Feure, Klimt, Klinger, Moreau, Redon, Rochegrosse, Rops, Stuck, and Toorop. Tolstoy mentions Klinger and Stuck in *What Is Art?* (translated by Aylmer Maude, 172).

78   *a manor serf* A serf taken from the land for service to the landlord in his household.

79   *the Polish right of veto* The doctor probably refers to the notorious *liberum veto,* or free veto, which was first used in the Sejm in 1652. Envoys or representatives could vote only according to their instructions from their provincial die-tines, or *sejmiki*. By using the veto, an envoy not only defeated the present motion, for which unanimity was required, but also annulled the proceedings of the current session of the Sejm, though usually one needed the support of several other envoys to wreck a session. This system was modified in 1768 and abolished by the constitution of May 3, 1791, but restored in a limited form in 1793.

79 *the second-person plural* This is to say that the guest uses the respectful form, like the French *vous*.

80 *the third-person plural* The housemaid uses the plural when speaking of Goga to show great respect, but this cannot be rendered in English. In "Divine and Human," section 1, the courier uses it when speaking of Ivan Matveevich.

83 *in the front corner* Where the icons were placed.

Appendix

91 *Ovruch (in Volhynia)* Ovruch is by the Norin River in northern Ukraine; Volhynia was a province.

92 *Presnovskaya stanitsa* A *stanitsa* was a large Cossack vil-lage. Presnovka is in North Kazakhstan Oblast (district), west of Petropavlovsk.

93 *Ust–Kamenogorsk fortress* In East Kazakhstan Oblast on the right bank of the Irtysh.

93 *Verkhneudinsk* Ulan-Ude.

94 *Nerchinsk mines* Nerchinsk is in Transbaikalia. At Ner-chinskii Zavod (works), which is east of Nerchinsk and close to the Chinese border, there were lead and silver mines and foundries. Here were the main Siberian hard-labor camps.

95   *secundum*   In the 1871 edition of *Sibir i Katorga* this is wrongly printed as *secundam*. This mistake is repeated in "What For?" according to the 1987 edition of Tolstoy's collected works.

96   *kościół*   A Polish Roman Catholic church.

96   *the wedding . . . emperor*   Alexander II, who was emperor at the time of the first publication of *Siberia and Penal Servitude*, had married Marie of Hessen-Darmstadt on April 16, 1841.

Note Sources

The historical and geographic information in the translator's notes to the stories and appendix is taken from the following sources:

Hingley, Ronald. *Nihilists: Russian Radicals and Revolutionaries in the Reign of Alexander II (1855–81)*. London: Weidenfeld and Nicolson, 1967.

———. *The Tsars: Russian Autocrats, 1533–1917*. London: Weidenfeld and Nicolson, 1968.

Jullian, Philippe. *Dreamers of Decadence: Symbolist Painters of the 1890s*. 2d ed. London: Phaidon, 1974.

Keep, John L. H. *Soldiers of the Tsar: Army and Society in Russia, 1462–1874*. Oxford: Clarendon Press, 1985.

Leslie, R. F. *Polish Politics and the Revolution of November 1830*. London: Athlone Press, University of London, 1956.

Lincoln, W. Bruce. *In War's Dark Shadow: The Russians before the Great War*. New York: Dial Press, 1983.

———. *The Romanovs: Autocrats of All the Russias*. London: Weidenfeld and Nicolson, 1981.

Lukowski, Jerzy. *Liberty's Folly: The Polish-Lithuanian Commonwealth in the Eighteenth Century, 1697–1795*. London and New York: Routledge, 1991.

Pipes, Richard. *Russia under the Old Regime*. London: Weidenfeld and Nicolson, 1974.

Prokhorov, A. M., ed. *Great Soviet Encyclopedia*. Translation of the 3d ed. 32 vols. New York: Collier Macmillan, 1973–83.

Pushkin, A. S. *Kapitanskaya Dochka*. Notes and vocabulary by V. Korotky and K. Villiers. Moscow: Progress, n.d.

Reddaway, W. F., J. H. Penson, O. Halecki, and R. Dyboski, eds. *The Cambridge History of Poland from Augustus II to Pilsudski (1697–1935)*. Cambridge: Cambridge University Press, 1941.

Rogger, Hans. *Russia in the Age of Modernisation and Revolution, 1881–1917*. London and New York: Longman, 1983.

Sochava, V. B., ed. *Atlas Zabaikalya (Buryatskaya ASSR i Chitinskaya Oblast)*. Moscow and Irkutsk: Glavnoe Upravlenie Geodezii i Kartografii pri Sovete Ministrov SSSR, 1967.

Starkov, V., and V. Filatov, eds. *Atlas: Russia and the Post-Soviet Republics*. Hastings, East Sussex: Arguments and Facts Media, 1994.

Tolstoi, L. N. *Sobranie Sochinenii v Dvenadtsati Tomakh*. Edited by S. A. Makashin and L. D. Opulskaya. Vol. 11. Moscow: Pravda, 1987.

Venturi, Franco. *Roots of Revolution: A History of the Populist and Socialist Movements in Nineteenth-Century Russia*. Translated from the Italian by Francis Haskell. Introduction by Isaiah Berlin. London: Weidenfeld and Nicolson, 1960.

Walicki, Andrzej. *A History of Russian Thought from the Enlightenment to Marxism*. Translated from the Polish by Hilda Andrews-Rusiecka. Stanford: Stanford University Press, 1979.

Wandycz, Piotr S. *The Lands of Partitioned Poland, 1795–1918*. Seattle and London: University of Washington Press, 1974.

Wood, Alan. *The Origins of the Russian Revolution, 1861–1917*. 2d ed. London and New York: Routledge, 1993.

European Classics

M. Ageyev
Novel with Cocaine

Jerzy Andrzejewski
Ashes and Diamonds

Honoré de Balzac
The Bureaucrats

Andrei Bely
Kotik Letaev

Heinrich Böll
Absent without Leave
And Never Said a Word
And Where Were You, Adam?
The Bread of Those Early Years
End of a Mission
Irish Journal
Missing Persons and Other Essays
The Safety Net
A Soldier's Legacy
The Stories of Heinrich Böll
Tomorrow and Yesterday
The Train Was on Time
What's to Become of the Boy?
Women in a River Landscape

Madeleine Bourdouxhe
La Femme de Gilles

Karel Čapek
Nine Fairy Tales
War with the Newts

Lydia Chukovskaya
Sofia Petrovna

Grazia Deledda
After the Divorce
Elias Portolu

Leonid Dobychin
The Town of N

Yury Dombrovsky
The Keeper of Antiquities

Aleksandr Druzhinin
Polinka Saks • The Story
of Aleksei Dmitrich

Venedikt Erofeev
Moscow to the End of the Line

Konstantin Fedin
Cities and Years

Arne Garborg
Weary Men

Fyodor Vasilievich Gladkov
Cement

I. Grekova
The Ship of Widows

Vasily Grossman
Forever Flowing

Stefan Heym
The King David Report

Marek Hlasko
The Eighth Day of the Week

Bohumil Hrabal
Closely Watched Trains

Ilf and Petrov
The Twelve Chairs

Vsevolod Ivanov
Fertility and Other Stories

Erich Kästner
Fabian: The Story of a Moralist

Valentine Kataev
Time, Forward!

Kharms and Vvedensky
The Man with the Black Coat:
Russia's Literature of the Absurd

Danilo Kiš
The Encyclopedia of the Dead
Hourglass

Ignacy Krasicki
The Adventures of Mr. Nicholas
Wisdom

Miroslav Krleza
The Return of Philip Latinowicz

Curzio Malaparte
Kaputt
The Skin

Karin Michaëlis
The Dangerous Age

Neera
Teresa

V. F. Odoevsky
Russian Nights

Andrey Platonov
The Foundation Pit

Bolesław Prus
The Sins of Childhood and
Other Stories

Valentin Rasputin
Farewell to Matyora

Alain Robbe-Grillet
Snapshots

Arthur Schnitzler
The Road to the Open

Yury Trifonov
Another Life and The House on the
Embankment
Disappearance
The Old Man

Evgeniya Tur
Antonina

Ludvík Vaculík
The Axe

Vladimir Voinovich
The Life and Extraordinary Adventures
of Private Ivan Chonkin
Pretender to the Throne

Stefan Zeromski
The Faithful River

Lydia Zinovieva-Annibal
The Tragic Menagerie

Stefan Zweig
Beware of Pity